CLIPPED WINGS

PARADISE CRIME MYSTERIES NOVELLA 4.5

TOBY NEAL

"So now faith, hope, and love abide, these three; but the greatest of these is love."

~ 1 Corinthians 13:13

CHAPTER ONE

CONSUELO

Morning glowed through steel wire embedded in the glass of the youth correctional facility's high window. Consuelo Aguilar lay on her back, gazing up at a Jack Canfield quote she'd written out and taped to the bottom of the bunk above her. *"Everything you want is on the other side of fear."*

Only today, everything she wanted was on the other side of barbed wire.

There was no point in getting up. Lying here was probably the most comfortable she'd be all day, and if she got up, she might wake Fai.

She could hear Fai's deep, rhythmic snores. The Tongan girl was never in a good mood when she woke up.

Consuelo could just see the waving top of a palm tree through the tiny window, its fronds backlit and black against the dawn sky. "That's how I feel. Backlit and black," she whispered. She rolled over and reached under the bunk for her notebook and pen, and jotted the phrase into the notebook.

Doing so felt as vain as writing the words in sand on the beach —as if they'd blow away the minute she lifted the pen from the paper—but writing was part of her therapy. Part of her future. If she ever had one . . .

Consuelo set the notebook back down and gazed at the picture of Angel, her teacup Chihuahua, right beneath the Canfield quote.

She was going to see Angel soon, when Special Agent Lei Texeira, her mentor, brought the little dog to visit. It was important to remember all the things she had to live for, even if some of the most important were already gone.

"That's the depression talking," Consuelo muttered. Dr. Wilson, her therapist, was always reminding her that the depression had its own voice, and fighting it began with identifying its insidious lies.

Fai snorted and turned over, making the bed's old metal springs squeak. "What'chu talking down deah?" she growled.

"Notting," Consuelo said.

Their voices held the lilt of pidgin, a dialect of Hawaii. Fai wasn't a friend, but at least she hadn't been an enemy. The Tongan girl could deadlift two hundred pounds, her homemade tattoos writhing up her arms and thighs. Sometimes she liked to show off by cracking *kukui* nuts in the exercise yard with her bare feet.

No one messed with Fai. Having her as a roommate had kept Consuelo out of many of the girl fights.

So. What was on the other side of fear?

Flying. Being free.

Folding her hands under her head, Consuelo let her mind drift back to when she'd been flying in her stolen plane, free as a dove.

For a while, she'd gone anywhere she'd wanted to. Taken anything she wanted. She hadn't used what she'd taken for herself. She'd stolen from the rich and given it to those who needed it. *She'd made a difference.* For a little while, she'd been a hero.

It sucked to lie here and remember how that had felt.

Depression talking again.

She was going to have a life when she got out of here. Her mentors, Lei Texeira, the FBI agent who captured her, and Wendy

Watanabe, the reporter who'd covered her case, had made sure of it. In fact, she owed them, big-time. Wendy had raised money to hire Bennie Fernandez, the state's top-notch defense lawyer, and Lei had helped her get mental health help. Between the two of them, Consuelo was only in the correctional facility for two years.

"You like get out of here?" Fai's husky voice seemed to read her thoughts.

"What you mean, Fai?"

"What'chu think I mean?"

"I don't know." Consuelo cautiously threw back the thin blue synthetic blanket and sheet, all that was necessary for warmth in the tropical climate. She swung her legs out of the low bunk and peered up at the other girl.

Fai's round brown face, her thick black hair a tangled halo, looked down. "We going get out of here. Early." Fai's dark brown eyes were hard as pebbles. "You can come."

Consuelo's heart pounded in heavy thuds that filled her ears. "I'm just doing my time. I only have two years."

"I've already been here two years, and I sick of the bullshit." Fai scowled. "I want to leave before they send me to the federal facility on the Mainland. My uncle, he goin' set us up with IDs. My cousin, he get one boat. Taking me and Jadene to another island."

"Why're you telling me this?" Consuelo stood up, took a few steps away from the bunk to get a better look at her roommate.

"Because. If you come, and we get caught, we all get off easy. I not stupid." Fai sat up, her legs dangling off the bunk. She pulled the correctional-issue plain black tee down over her loose breasts and combed back thick, bushy hair with a tattooed hand. "You get the good lawyer. I getting some insurance for Jadene and me." Jadene, a white trash *haole* girl from Kaneohe, was Fai's current girlfriend.

"It doesn't work that way." Consuelo felt her mouth go dry. "Ask my boyfriend. He got twice my time." Her boyfriend was

3

captured at the same time and was serving a much longer sentence at a facility in Utah.

"Dat boy was over eighteen, as' why. You do this, you going give all those rich assholes the finger. Just like you was doing before you got caught. You got one whole movement going on the outside, I been hearing." Fai's eyes gleamed with excitement.

It had been two months since Consuelo had been released from Tripler Hospital's mental health ward and begun her sentence at Oahu Youth Correctional Facility, and this was the first time Fai had indicated she knew or cared about Consuelo's public past.

"I need to think about it. What's the plan?" Consuelo pulled the plain black sleep tee off over her head, clipped on her bra, and zipped up her orange coverall.

Fai jumped down from the top bunk, landing with a thump beside her. "Not telling you unless you're in."

"I can't agree until I hear the plan." Consuelo had her back to the other girl as she stowed her sleep tee in the cheap cardboard bureau where their clothes were stored.

Fai threw a meaty arm around Consuelo's neck, hauling her up against her heavy, muscular body in a chokehold, with Consuelo's head caught in the crook of her elbow. She pushed Consuelo's head forward with her other hand as she lifted the much smaller Filipina girl off her feet, cutting off her air supply. "You no tell me notting, *chica*."

Consuelo heaved and thrashed, clawing at Fai's arm. She kicked back at Fai's legs with her unshod feet, but the bigger girl merely grunted, twisting so that Consuelo dangled off her hip. Consuelo's flailing had no effect at all.

"You think you're all that," the older girl hissed in her ear. "You nothing but a flea. I could kill you right now. And I will, if you say one word about this. You're coming with us."

She flung Consuelo like a doll. The petite girl flew forward and hit the wall, sliding down to the floor in a gasping heap.

Black spots gradually receded from Consuelo's vision as she

caught her breath. She pulled herself together and sat up, drawing her knees close against her chest, touching her bruised throat.

There was nothing to be done at the moment but play along. Fai was right. She'd be dead anytime the girl wanted to kill her.

Fai turned away as if nothing had happened. She dressed in her prison orange, humming a little as she dragged a comb through her thick hair.

Consuelo's voice was hoarse as she said, "I guess I'm coming."

CHAPTER TWO

ROSARIO

Rosario Texeira smoothed her plumeria-print apron down over the sensible sweats she wore with chef's clogs. She washed her hands at the industrial-sized sink, her gaze flicking around the kitchen with its adjoining dishwasher station, unconsciously cataloguing and making a mental note of spices that needed refilling, cracks and corners that needed scrubbing. Not for the first time, she counted herself blessed not to have to keep the restaurant open for a dinner shift, as well.

But now wasn't the time for kitchen cleaning—she had a teenaged busboy coming in to help her with that after he finished school for the day. Before he did, she had an important weekly chore to complete—one that always filled her with satisfaction. Time to do the food inventory so she could order for the week.

Rosario dried her hands on a clean white towel and took the order sheet on its clipboard off of the metal rack that held her favorite pots and pans, and headed for the walk-in refrigerator.

She pulled open the heavy steel door of the walk-in, and parted the dangling plastic panels that helped keep the cold inside. As she stepped through, she inhaled deeply, taking in the rich smells of ginger, onions, garlic, and fresh vegetables, with overtones of the tropical fruits that were a unique part of Hawaiian cooking. She stepped forward on the raised rubber flooring with its round holes for traction and drainage, and examined the rack of metal shelves that lined the chilly room.

She had established an order of storage for the items, so it was a fairly rapid process to check how many eggs and how much butter, cheese, salad dressing, sauces, fruits and greens she had.

Rosario and her brother Wayne had grown up poor on the Big Island. They were the surviving offspring of a Portuguese *paniolo* 'Hawaiian cowboy' on a big Waimea estate, and his Hawaiian wife, their beloved Mama, who'd cleaned and cooked for the family that owned the ranch. Wayne had taken to the *paniolo* life-style in his father's footsteps, while Rosario had learned her mother's skills in cooking and estate management.

Their parents had died in a car wreck when she and her brother were in their late teens, and Rosario had moved to California, hoping to build a better life for herself—which she had done in working her way up to into establishing *Aunty's Hawaiian Food Place* with her partner, Momi.

Rosario ticked down her order sheet on autopilot, her mind drifting back to the ways that life had taken dark turns: her brother Wayne and his wife Maylene falling into drugs. Maylene's death by overdose while Wayne was incarcerated, which had brought their feisty daughter Lei to live with Rosario at age nine.

Her niece Lei had had a traumatic and abuse-filled childhood that had left her with lasting scars, but Lei had come so far in overcoming her past that she was now an FBI agent on Oahu.

And with any luck at all, she'd be coming to her aunt's for Christmas this year.

Rosario inhaled the smell of baby new potatoes, parsley, mint, and ginger in their boxes, instinctively sniffing for anything spoiled.

There was—a small red potato with a spot of black rot. Rosario extracted the offending tuber from the box and opened the square, sealed bin where she stored spoiling food and leftovers from the restaurant to feed to pigs at a friend's farm, in trade for a supply of fresh pork.

Her eyebrows rose as she dropped the spoiled potato into the bin.

It should be nearly full after three days. She had the waitstaff scrape plates into a special garbage bag, and then deposit it in the bin along with any expired, unsold food from the stand of convenience foods Rosario kept stocked at the counter. Several bags of leftover food and a half dozen expired hard-boiled eggs, along with some papayas and avocados she'd bought for garnishes that had been overripe, should be in the bin.

But there were only two eggs, no papayas or avocados, and a couple of white plastic bags of leftovers.

Rosario was the one to take the bin to the pig farm twice a week; who would take food meant for the animals?

Maybe the scraps had been mislaid somehow.

Her attention sharpening, Rosario did another inventory, quickly checking through the entire contents of the walk-in.

The refrigerator's chill began to set in, working its way through her layers of clothing, and Rosario shivered as the walk-in door opened, gently blowing the plastic panels apart to reveal her busboy, sixteen-year-old Josef.

"Josef, some food's missing from the bin. Do you know what might have happened to it?"

The boy's eyebrows rose. "No, Aunty. Who would take your pig slops?"

"I know, that's what's so weird." Rosario chewed the end of her pen, staring down into the bin. "I think this has been going on for a while, but this is the first time I'm absolutely certain there's something missing. I really noticed the papayas and avocadoes because I hated to throw them out; they only had a few spots, but they wouldn't do for the garnishes I had in mind."

Josef shook his head, his messy hair flopping to and fro. "I don't know, Aunty. We should ask the staff. Maybe someone has a dog or something."

Rosario shrugged. "Well, no big deal. It was going to the pigs anyway. But I will check and see if anyone knows anything. Can you get started on scrubbing down the big grill while I put in the food order on the computer?"

"Of course, Aunty." Josef spoke English very well for a second language; he'd told Rosario he'd come to the U.S. from Mexico with his family when he was five. He disappeared back through the transparent panels.

Rosario followed Josef's straight, slender height out of the walk-in, and shut the door with a substantial thump. "Help yourself to some chocolate macadamia nut cookies and a Coke," Rosario told him, as she often did. "You're too skinny and you're a growing boy."

"Gracias. Soon as I'm done with the grill." Josef put on heavy gloves and picked up a steel wool pad as he approached the big iron grill. The light shone on his hair, and her fingers itched to scissor it into shape. "You're too good to me, Aunty."

Rosario slung an arm around Josef's shoulders to give the teen an awkward side hug. "You work so hard. You deserve a few perks."

Then she went into Momi's office to place the weekly food order. Her business partner was behind the computer, as usual, but got up to surrender her seat so that Rosario could key in the order from their suppliers.

Momi was a tall, statuesque Hawaiian woman who dressed in classic muumuus and wore a fresh gardenia behind her ear every day that she could get one. She sat in their spare chair and pulled out the crochet project she was working on, baby booties for a grandbaby soon to arrive.

Rosario told her partner about the missing food. "So weird. Who would take plate scrapings and old food?"

"Maybe Jenny took it; she has one of those silly Vietnamese potbellied pigs at home," Momi said.

Rosario nodded, relieved. "I bet that's it."

She began entering her food order, but a few minutes later Momi said, "You know, I think someone is getting into my office, too."

Rosario's fingers paused on the keyboard. "What do you mean?"

Momi pointed her crochet hook at the bags of flour, coffee beans, taro roots and rice piled up against the wall next to a stack of folded empty fabric sacks. "Sometimes when I come in, the bags look like they've been moved. And there were crumbs on the floor."

"What?" Rosario's voice rose. "Was anything missing?" Both of their gazes flew to the sturdy, wall-mounted safe behind the desk, hidden under a photo of the restaurant.

"No. Nothing's missing. The safe is untouched. I figured someone must have been coming in here on their break and eating. I've been keeping the door locked all the time I'm not in here, but it's still happening."

The women exchanged a long glance. "I think I better ask Lei what to do," Rosario said. "We have a mystery on our hands."

Momi laughed her rich, comfortable chuckle. "A burglar who eats our poi rolls. The crumbs I saw were purple."

"I threw out a batch that got burned," Rosario said. "Put them in the pig bin. But come to think of it, they weren't there when I took the bin to the farm earlier this week."

"Someone's definitely helping themselves to the bin, then. But do we really care about that?" Momi quirked one of her elegant brows.

Rosario put a hand on a hip. "Sure, we do! I need those scraps for the farm, to make sure we get a good ration of fresh pork at slaughtering time."

Momi shuddered. "I prefer to think our meat floats down from heaven wrapped in plastic."

"You're just lucky I don't ask for a whole pig and make an *imu* out back to cook it all myself," Rosario said.

"Good thing we only have a cement parking lot back there with no room for an underground oven, because I wouldn't put it past you."

Jenny, a pretty twentysomething cousin of Momi's from the Big Island, stuck her head in. "Got my paycheck, Aunty?" Everyone on staff called both women "aunty" as a title of respect, tradition in Hawaii with senior female relatives.

"Got your check right here." Momi dug an envelope out of the green cashbox on her desk and handed it over to Jenny.

Rosario swiveled her office chair to face the girl. "You been taking our scraps home to that pet pig of yours?"

Jenny straightened in surprise. "No, Aunty. I wouldn't do that without asking."

Momi and Rosario glanced at each other, frowning, and Jenny took that opportunity to disappear.

"Someone is stealing from our walk-in," Rosario said.

"The mystery of the missing pig slops. Stay tuned, film at eleven," Momi deadpanned, and Rosario finally smiled—but it bugged her that someone in their *ohana* of trusted staff was taking without asking.

CHAPTER THREE

CONSUELO

Consuelo hid her hands in the loose pockets of her orange coverall as she walked into the visiting area. She kept her face still, so as not to reveal the dread and excitement that filled her that her mentor, Special Agent Lei Texeira, was here to visit, bringing Consuelo's dog, Angel.

The two came every week, but due to Lei's busy FBI work schedule, it was never a predictable day or time. Consuelo hated to admit how much she looked forward to the sight of the curly-haired brunette agent with the warm, tilted brown eyes and smatter of freckles on her nose—but she didn't have to hide how happy she was to see Angel.

The little Chihuahua, wearing a tiny therapy dog vest, bounced toward Consuelo, yipping with excitement. Consuelo scooped the dog up, ducking her head to hide her emotion.

"Hey, baby," she whispered into Angel's sleek neck. The little animal wagged her curly tail, her whole body vibrating. She licked Consuelo's neck, and Consuelo tossed her head back and laughed.

"Consuelo." Lei's voice was brusque. "Come here."

"Yes?" Consuelo turned to Lei, her heart pounding.

They weren't alone in the room. Knots of girls visited with their families around the bolted-down tables. In a far corner, Fai and Jadene were twined together on one of the couches. Consuelo felt the older girls' eyes burning a hole in her coverall as she advanced to sit on one of the metal stools beside Lei.

Usually Lei let Consuelo play with Angel alone for a few minutes, or let the other girls who still hadn't really warmed up to Consuelo pet the little dog. Today, the agent's gaze was intent and probing. "I need to speak to you privately."

"Okay." Consuelo moved to a stool right next to Lei, holding the dog in her arms. She still hadn't decided if she was going to go along with Fai's planned breakout, or if she was going to try to tell someone and get it stopped. Either choice was fraught with risk. She felt herself teetering on the brink of the hard choice as she gazed into Lei's concerned brown eyes.

"There's a bruise on your neck." Lei pushed a hank of Consuelo's glossy black hair away. "On both sides of your neck."

Consuelo shrugged. "It's no big deal."

"Hey. Who's your friend?" Fai's voice came from over Consuelo's shoulder, and she felt the Tongan's bulk behind her.

Consuelo kept her face neutral and her voice flat. "This is Special Agent Lei Texeira. With the FBI."

"You get visits from cops?" Fai's meaty hand came down to rest on Consuelo's shoulder and squeezed.

"Back up off of Consuelo." Lei's voice cracked with authority, though the agent hadn't moved from her stool.

Fai's hand loosened and slid away. Her tone was sulky. "Introduce me, roomie."

"Agent Texeira, this is Fai Afa. My roommate." And this time, when Consuelo raised her eyes to Lei, she knew her expression was pleading. Much as she was tempted by the opportunity to escape, she wanted more than anything to have this awful dilemma taken from her.

"Is this girl threatening you?" Lei's gaze seemed to bore into Consuelo's. She switched her frown to Fai.

Consuelo riffled through her choices mentally as she stroked the Chihuahua snuggled up to her shoulder. "No. We're friends," Consuelo said. "Fai's helped me a lot in here. Kept the bullies away." This was perfectly true.

Fai patted Consuelo's back in an approximation of friendly approval. "That's right. No one messes with my friends."

Jadene approached. "I've noticed you every week when you come," the skinny blonde said to Lei. Consuelo's stomach turned at the girl's shy act, so falsely sincere. "It's great how someone important like you takes care of Consuelo's dog."

The two girls hovered nearby for the duration of Lei's visit, taking turns petting Angel and making it impossible to get a moment alone with the agent. Lei seemed to be buying the girls' friendly act, and Consuelo's stomach tightened at the thought of how her mentor would feel when she heard of the trio's escape. *Lei would feel betrayed.*

Consuelo knew how betrayal felt.

She didn't want to ruin what she had with Lei. The situation squeezed her like the tightening coils of a boa constrictor.

Lei smiled at the other girls. "Can I get a moment alone with Consuelo? News of her family."

Consuelo had no family, but Fai and Jadene didn't know that. Fai gave Consuelo a last glance over her shoulder, and the two moved off.

Lei leaned forward, petting Angel, who'd fallen asleep with all the attention and now snoozed in the crook of Consuelo's arm.

"Is there something you need to tell me?" Lei's voice was soft. A fall of her curly dark-brown hair hid her lips from the prying eyes that Consuelo could feel at her back.

"I'd like a different roommate," Consuelo whispered. "As soon as possible."

"I'll see what I can do," Lei whispered back.

Consuelo felt a weight lift. She wasn't going to have to deal with this situation if she could just get moved out of Fai's room.

It was an emotional wrench when she said goodbye to Lei and Angel, but there was a little more spring in her walk as she left the visiting area. Maybe Lei could get her away from Fai before the breakout.

Fai caught her in the hall on their way to their room, hooking an arm around Consuelo's bruised neck in a parody of friendship that the nearby correctional officer, a big mixed Hawaiian woman they called Aunty Marcie, didn't react to.

"How's your family?" Fai asked, giving Consuelo a little push into their room.

"Fine." Consuelo tried to get some distance. The door was kept open except at night, and even then, the COs checked on the girls periodically through the wire-covered viewing window.

Fai followed Consuelo in, crowding her. "You were pretty cozy with that agent."

Consuelo had had enough. She whirled toward the bigger girl. "Leave me alone," she hissed. "I said I'd go. I didn't say anything to Lei, even though she asked me if I was okay. I kept your secret, and I'm going along with your plan. Leave me the hell alone. You keep hassling me, and someone's going to realize something's up."

"What's the problem here?" Aunty Marcie boomed from the doorway.

Consuelo, hands on her hips, glared up at the big Tongan and didn't look away. "Everything's fine, Aunty Marcie," she said.

Fai took a step back, turned to face Aunty Marcie with a smile that showed her straight, white teeth. "This girl. She keeps trying to borrow my panties."

Aunty Marcie gave a snort of laughter at that unlikely scenario. She watched a minute longer, but Consuelo just climbed into her bunk and reached for her notebook as Fai sat down at the little desk with one of her community college textbooks.

Turned toward the wall, Consuelo opened her notebook and uncapped her pen.

She finally had an idea of what she could do to help herself.

CHAPTER FOUR

LEI

Lei held up her cred wallet at the exit sally port so that the guard could see it. "I need to speak to the warden." She'd thought over her visit with Consuelo. There was no doubt something was wrong, and Lei hadn't needed Consuelo's whispered request for a new roommate to tell her that it had something to do with the big Tongan girl and her blonde sidekick.

The security agent nodded and picked up the phone. A few minutes later, a correctional officer opened the door. "Right this way, ma`am."

Lei grimaced as she followed the stocky CO down the hall. *At what point had she crossed that invisible age line into 'ma'am?'*

Efforts had been made, in this area at least, to soften the look of the youth facility. Artwork by the girls decorated the walls. An incomplete hand-painted mural gave a sense of something abandoned, as so many of the kids were.

Lei had taken a moment to put Angel back in the car with the windows down before returning to speak to the warden.

The warden was an older Caucasian man wearing Hawaii business casual: a muted aloha shirt and chinos. A ring of keys and an ID badge bounced above his belt buckle as he strode toward Lei.

"I'm Grover Smith. How can I help the FBI today?" The man's weathered skin crinkled around blue eyes faded by years of squinting. *Sailor or golfer*, Lei guessed as she shook his hand.

"I'm here on behalf of Consuelo Aguilar," Lei said.

"Ah, our famous guest," Smith said. "What's she done now?"

Lei smiled politely. "As you may know from the media, I was the one to capture and bring Consuelo in. I've been—mentoring her, shall we say, and it appears that there's a problem with her roommate."

"So. You're not here in an official capacity." The smiley crinkles disappeared from Smith's face. "The internal affairs of the youth facility are none of the FBI's business."

"I realize that, of course." Lei's heart rate spiked with irritation, but she made an open gesture with her hands. Hard lessons in the past had taught her not to show emotions to these bureaucrat types. "I believe Consuelo's being intimidated by her roommate. There could be trouble. I just thought I'd give you a heads-up that Wendy Watanabe, of KHIN-2, also has an interest in Consuelo and could pop by at any time. She's told me she's thinking of doing an in-depth piece on the facility."

Smith glared, hands on his hips. "You can't blackmail me with media pressure. Aguilar gets no preferential treatment. It sets a bad precedent."

"There has never been, nor likely ever will be, another case like Consuelo Aguilar," Lei said tightly. "Consuelo's not one to complain, but she asked me to help her get another roommate. I wouldn't be here if I didn't think it meant that something serious was going on."

"I'll take it under advisement. Now, if there's nothing else . . ." Smith wasn't going to budge.

"No. You've been very unhelpful, and it's duly noted." Lei

spun on her heel and headed outside. *No point in any further social niceties.*

At her truck, Lei petted Angel as she thumbed through the contacts on her phone to find Wendy Watanabe's personal cell. She and the petite anchorwoman would never be friends, but they'd come to a mutual respect for each other over several cases—and a shared interest in the brave teen who'd captured both of their hearts.

"Texeira. To what do I owe the pleasure?" Watanabe's voice was crisp.

"I'm at Oahu Youth Correctional Facility. Consuelo's got a problem with her roommate. Big Tongan girl named Fai Afa. I'm going to look into Afa's criminal background, but I thought you might be interested in the fact that Warden Smith blew off my warning of a problem and Consuelo's request for another roommate."

"Jerk." Lei could almost see the narrowing of Watanabe's almond-shaped, sharp brown eyes. "I wasn't kidding. I want to do a story on that place. I've heard some nasty rumors."

"This might not be a bad time to poke around. I have a feeling our girl's in trouble. She wouldn't tell me more, but for her to ask me for help . . ."

"Yeah. I'm on it." Watanabe hung up with a brisk click.

Satisfied for the moment, Lei started her vehicle. "Gotta run background on Afa and her friend," she told Angel. "But it's late. Let's get home and relax first."

LEI UNSLUNG her backpack that doubled as a purse and hung it on the hook inside of her door, as Angel and Keiki greeted each other ecstatically.

Lei's boyfriend Stevens had brought Lei's big Rottweiler over to Oahu when they'd reconciled a few months prior. Lei enjoyed the contrast of the tiny, aggressive teacup Chihuahua with Keiki's massive but peaceful presence. The two dogs usually slept curled up together in Keiki's bed, and combined, were better than a doorbell and an armed alarm system. Lei fed them side by side, smiling at the sight of their similarly marked but completely different shapes as the two greedily crunched through their kibble.

Lei headed for her bedroom and shed her wrinkled FBI "uniform" of linen jacket, shoulder holster, plain white button-down shirt, gray slacks, socks, shoes, belt, badge, and small, six shot revolver ankle rig. She hung her weapons in their usual place on the spindle at the corner of the bed, then took a shower.

The dogs were waiting at her bathroom door when she got out, eager for their evening romp in her postage-stamp of fenced yard. "You two aren't too subtle, are you?" she teased, squashing some product into her curly hair in hopes that it would be manageable tomorrow.

Keiki whined, and Angel hopped up on her hind legs and danced in a circle, making Lei laugh.

The sound almost startled her, and she realized it was the first time she'd laughed in days. That was sad. She addressed the dogs. "That's what you girls are good for. Comic relief from life's piles of nasty crap."

Consuelo's worried face rose in her mind's eye: the girl's full mouth tight with secrets, her eyes shadowed with fear.

"We've got to get something better for Consuelo," Lei muttered as she unlocked the front door and let the dogs out into the yard. She was glad the girl had Bennie Fernandez and Wendy Watanabe to defend her, too. Maybe between the three of them, they could get Consuelo moved to a better, safer facility . . . Lei poured herself a glass of chardonnay, filled a bowl with tortilla chips and carrot sticks, and went outside onto the porch.

The dogs were doing their usual sniff-and-pee around the small yard with its high wooden fence lined with night blooming jasmine and honeysuckle. The flowers' sweetness filled the cooling air of a late fall Honolulu evening, along with a chorus of squawking from a nearby mango tree in the neighbors' yard, where a flock of mynah birds gathered in the evenings to gossip.

Lei grabbed a crocheted shawl Aunty Rosario had made, and took out her old relic of a flip phone. She opened it and pressed down a *Favorites* button whose digit was worn off with use, as she settled herself into one of a pair of old rattan chairs on her little lanai.

"Sweets! Long time since you called your aunty!" Rosario had a warm, rich voice to go along with a face creased by smiles and time as she called Lei by her family nickname. Her aunt's dimpled cheeks, long silver-streaked hair and bright brown eyes were vivid in Lei's mind's eye.

"How you doing, Aunty?" Lei slipped easily into pidgin. "I been missing you, too. And that yummy pineapple upside-down cake you make."

"Good, good, Momi and I, we both good. And I'm making that pineapple cake this weekend, along with some of that beef stew you like and those purple poi rolls I always run out of."

"Oh, Aunty, you know how to make me homesick!" Lei exclaimed. "Those are my favorites!"

"Well, you going make it for Christmas? I'll make all of your favorites!" Aunty wheedled.

Lei smiled, tucking the ends of the old shawl around her. "I'm coming. I put in for leave already."

She had to hold her phone away from her ear at the loud whoop of joy from her aunt. "Momi, my girl's coming home for Christmas!" Rosario hollered.

Momi got on the phone for greetings, and finally Lei had her aunt back on the line. "I can't wait to see you," Rosario said. "But honey, I get one small problem. Maybe you can help."

"Anything, Aunty." Rosario had never married or had children. She'd rescued Lei from the jaws of the foster care system when Lei's mother had died, after locking Lei in their garage. Lei would never have grown into the woman she was now without her aunt's steady, unconditional love—and she knew it to her bones.

Maylene might have given Lei life, but Rosario had given Lei *a life*.

"Food is going missing from the walk-in fridge. We have an alarm on the front and back doors of the restaurant, so I don't know who or how the food is disappearing. What I can do?"

"Did you ever get a smartphone, Aunty?"

"Of course. Only you still using that old flip phone, Sweets," her aunt teased.

"I do have to use a smartphone for work, of course." Lei pulled her work phone out of her pocket. "There are these great little remote nanny cams you can buy that run off your phone. I'll buy some and have them shipped to you, okay? You just put them up where you want to watch something, and they'll detect motion and ping you on your phone, and you can see who's taking things."

"Oh, honey, that would be so good."

Lei could hear sizzling in the background, and pictured the big old-fashioned iron grill that Aunty used for most of the cooking on the restaurant's menu. "Whatchu making, Aunty?"

"I'm cooking up a hundred pieces of Spam for tomorrow's *musubi*. I always sell out of it at the counter." In addition to sit-down meals, the restaurant also kept a basket of easy to-go items for busy families to grab on their way out the door.

"I get one of those most days at the corner store," Lei said. "So *ono*." A delicious snack that had originated with Japanese sugar-cane workers in lieu of a sandwich in the fields, *musubi* were comprised of a tightly packed block of white rice with a slice of fried Spam on top, the whole thing wrapped in a flavorful sheet of thin, delicious *nori,* a paper like pounded seaweed. "The tourists have no idea how tasty they are."

"I know, and I love them too. But I'm still here at seven at night cooking Spam after the breakfast and lunch shift. Good thing I got my helper Josef coming in early tomorrow morning to put them all together before the restaurant opens. He one good kid. He comes and works from four thirty a.m. 'til it's time for school."

"That's pretty dedicated. How does he get into the building?"

"He has a key, and the code. But most of the waitstaff has that access, and he one good boy. I already asked him and he doesn't know where the missing food's going." Lei heard a *ding*. "That's the rice cooker. Before I hired Josef, I had to come in at four thirty every morning. Now I can roll in at seven like the queen of Sheba."

Lei laughed. "No one ever accused you of being lazy, Aunty. Sounds like you're lucky to have him."

"He's a hard worker," Rosario said affectionately. Calling someone a hard worker was her highest form of praise.

"Well, I'm glad you have the help," Lei said. "I've already used my work phone to order you those cameras. They should be there in a couple of days. Ask Momi if you have any trouble hooking them up." Momi did all of the organization of the restaurant and the bookkeeping, to free Aunty up to manage the food and cooking.

"Thank you, Sweets. You made my day now that I know you going come home for Christmas."

"And with any luck, I'll have a young friend with me." Lei took a sip of her chardonnay. "Consuelo's an amazing girl, but she's had it rough. I'm going to try to get special permission to bring her. I can't wait to see her bite into your mango bread, or some of those poi rolls."

"Bring anyone you like, Sweets. Okay, I'll look for those cameras. And soon we'll solve the mystery, thanks to my niece in the FBI!"

They said goodbye, and Lei ended the call, smiling. She sipped her wine and watched the dogs play, romping and jumping in the waning evening light. The night blooming jasmine slowly opened, and she shut her eyes and leaned her head back in her comfy chair to breathe in the incredible smell.

She was tired. Tomorrow was soon enough to do that research on Consuelo's roommate.

CHAPTER FIVE

CONSUELO

Consuelo started awake, her heart pounding. Fai was shaking her shoulder roughly.

"It's time." The older girl thrust a handful of clothing at her.

Despair swamped Consuelo even as adrenaline hit her system. *If Lei had tried to get her transferred, it hadn't happened quickly enough.* She climbed out of the bunk and changed into the nylon basketball shorts and tank top Fai handed her. The older girl had received a package yesterday, and gym clothing was allowed for when the girls had exercise time, so apparently Fai had obtained an extra set for Consuelo. The box had been opened by the COs, but they had missed the little extras Fai's uncle had included.

Both girls put the few things they wanted to keep into pillowcases; Consuelo packed the photo of Angel and the Canfield quote, a few old photos of her family, and her notebook.

"Yeah, don't you try to leave that notebook behind," Fai hissed. "I don't want you giving away any clues."

"I wouldn't," Consuelo said stiffly.

The only illumination was thin, milky moonlight coming in through the high window and an embedded night light the COs used for checking on the inmates. Fai opened the box from her package and tore open a large loaf of cellophane-wrapped banana bread. Boxes were X-rayed for metal or weapons, but only visually inspected after that. Packages were also sniffed by scent dogs, but the strong smell of banana bread must have thrown the dogs off, because inside the loaf were a plastic key and two vials.

"Now comes the tricky part," Fai whispered. Consuelo could tell the other girl was nervous by the tremble in her voice. The Tongan unscrewed the pointed caps of the vials and squeezed the contents into the crack adjacent to the door lock.

A combustible combination of acids, the chemicals began working as soon as they connected with each other. A thin wisp of toxic-smelling smoke wafted from the doorjamb.

Consuelo hid her face, breathing through the edge of her blanket and shutting her eyes against the fumes. Her mind ticked over the steps she'd taken, and what she could do next.

There hadn't been much, unfortunately.

A few minutes later, Fai grabbed her shoulder.

"I think it's ready." With no interior handle, there was no way to open the door but to push. Fai pushed.

The door gave a bit, but held.

"I don't think the acid ate all the way through the wood," Fai whispered harshly. "Come help me."

The two girls ended up running and throwing their weight against the door. The remaining resistance finally gave with a crack and squeal that sounded like a scream.

Once out in the hall, Fai in the lead, they hurried to the room where Jadene was locked in with her roommate. Both of those girls were awake. Fai used the plastic key on their door, and unlocked it.

At the last minute, Jadene and Fai turned on Jadene's room-mate, a sturdy local girl named Pua, and shoved her back in, locking her inside the room.

"Bitches!" Pua yelled. She pounded and screamed, but the walls and doors were fairly soundproof.

"We have to hurry now in case anyone hears her," Fai said. They ran down the hall. As had been arranged with one of the COs who owed Fai's uncle a favor, the door into the rec room was left unlocked. From there it was a simple matter to open the exterior door out into the yard.

There were surveillance cameras in the hall, the rec room, and on the yard, but Fai's uncle had also paid for the system to be down for maintenance. The girls trotted unchallenged across the yard, keeping to the shadows, to a chosen exit point in the shadow of one of the buildings.

Fai squatted down and dug in the soil just beneath the chain-link fence topped in coils of razor wire, and produced a pair of heavy wire cutters. Consuelo felt her chest tighten with stress and regret. She looked back around, her gaze desperately sweeping the dim yard.

She'd never expected them to get this far.

Fai began cutting the wire in a seam, Jadene prying the wire open further as the powerful girl made each cut.

Suddenly lights went on inside the main cinder block building, and a pulsing electronic alarm split the air.

"That stupid Pua," Jadene hissed. "I bet she got someone to come with all her carrying on."

Fai hunched her shoulders, throwing muscle into the cutting. "Almost there."

Consuelo looked back again, still hoping someone would stop them. One of the doors to the main hall flew open.

"Halt!" an amplified voice yelled, but Fai had made the opening big enough. She wriggled through, tearing the fabric of her shorts on the sharp wire. Jadene whirled and grabbed a handful of Consuelo's long hair, shoving her in front. "Get through there, bitch."

"No," Consuelo cried, grabbing the fence. "Help! Help me!"

Fai reached back through the hole and grabbed Consuelo, but

29

she struggled harder, desperation giving her strength as she writhed and twisted in the other girls' grips.

"No! I don't want to go!" she yelled. Jadene finally let go and dove through the hole into Fai's arms. The two older girls hit the ground, scrambled up, and ran for a black pickup truck Consuelo could just make out idling at the edge of the cleared area that marked the compound's boundary.

Consuelo fell to her knees and clasped her hands behind her head, watching the girls reach the truck, jump in, and speed off. The CO pursuing them reached her. He knocked her flat to the ground, cuffing her, then yanked her up roughly.

"Where did they go?" The head night watchman, Keone, was a heavyset man. He'd always been someone she avoided. All the unplanned running had winded him, and he puffed cigarette breath into her face. Consuelo felt his rage at being made to look incompetent. He shook her. "Tell me now!"

"I didn't want to break out! I tried to stay here. Please call my friend, Agent Texeira!" Consuelo cried.

"I'll call someone for you," Keone said, and backhanded her so hard that everything went black.

CHAPTER SIX

Consuelo

Consuelo awoke on a gurney trundling somewhere. She tried to sit up. Panic surged through her—*she was restrained at her feet and hands!* She was strapped down, hardly able to move.

"Help! Help me!" she screamed, thrashing. "Help!"

"You just hush that noise." The voice speaking to her was familiar—Aunty Marcie, who'd often been kind. "Calm down. I'm taking you to the infirmary."

Consuelo forced her muscles to relax as ceiling lights moved by overhead. Her cheek throbbed where Keone had hit her. Her scalp hurt from the other girls pulling her hair.

"Please call my friend Lei Texeira," she whispered to the CO. "Please. I left a note for her in my room. I was forced. I didn't want to go with them." They'd already wheeled into the infirmary. Consuelo turned her head, desperately tracking Aunty Marcie. "Please. I was forced!"

"Just relax," Aunty Marcie said. "You'll be fine."

Consuelo yelped as the medic stabbed her in the arm with a needle. A few minutes later, she slid into darkness.

DRY MOUTH and pounding in her head.

Consuelo sat up slowly, relieved to discover she was no longer restrained, and looked around.

As she'd expected, she was in the isolation unit.

This wasn't the first time she'd seen the inside of this little "shoebox" from hell. She'd got into a scuffle with some girls early on, and spent a few days in here before Fai became her protector.

She actually liked being alone. The worst thing about "the shoe" was not having her notebook.

Hopefully Marcie or someone else had found the note she'd left tucked into her bedding. The letter detailed the escape, what she knew about Fai's plans and family, and that she was being coerced.

But Keone hadn't seemed like he was listening, and she couldn't tell if Marcie had, either.

Consuelo looked around the cell. The bed was a single metal shelf covered in rubber that folded up to the wall. A toilet, and a sink beside it, filled in one corner. A paper cup rested on the rim of the sink. The walls were padded with berber-style carpet, both to keep inmates from injuring themselves and to deaden sound. The only illumination to the roughly six-by-ten-foot space was a wire-covered window near the ceiling, and a couple of embedded glow lights overhead.

Lying on the cot, Consuelo mentally reviewed the situation.

If Aunty Marcie didn't contact anyone for her, she could be stuck in here for weeks.

She had to pinch herself on the arm to keep from giving in to the wave of hopelessness that swept over her at the thought. She'd made it through that dark time in the psych hospital by focusing on the things she had to live for, and that would stand her in good stead now, too.

She might be all alone with hardly any family, but she had friends.

Powerful friends.

And she had information, too. She'd gleaned all she could about Fai and her gangster uncles. They were connected with the notorious Boyz organized crime operation that controlled the construction trade in Honolulu.

If she could get someone to listen to her, she might be able to help get them stopped.

Lying there, Consuelo daydreamed about the book proposal her lawyer, Bennie Fernandez, had told her about a few weeks ago.

"HarperCollins wants to publish your memoir," the cherubic little lawyer had said, polishing his round glasses. "The conditions of you getting a reduced sentence include that you have to pay back all the property damage you caused. If you write the memoir, you might be able to achieve that, and still have a little something left over for when you get out of here."

"How much are they offering?" Consuelo felt a little queasy at the thought of having to put into words the complex reasons that had driven her to steal a small airplane and begin a Robin Hood-style crime spree. Even though she hadn't been involved with the destruction that had followed, she still felt responsible for that, and for the lives her actions had ended up costing. She'd been dealing with the whole situation by focusing on right now, surviving her life in prison.

"It's an advance of a hundred thousand, which is only a drop in the bucket to all the property damage caused by the anarchy movement you launched," Fernandez said. "I'm arguing that you can only be held responsible for the houses you burgled."

"Thanks for that," Consuelo said. "I want a chance to set the record straight. I might have been the one who started something, but I never meant it to end the way it did. I just wanted to draw attention to the gap between the rich and the poor in Hawaii."

"Well, you certainly did that." Fernandez set his glasses on his little pink bulb of a nose. "But I'd hate for that message to get lost in all that came after. I think you should do the memoir."

Lying on the bunk, without so much as a blanket, let alone pen and paper, depression and despair swept over her.

Consuelo shut her eyes.

She'd never be able to tell her story, or do anything to fight guys like Jose Taika, Fai's gangster uncle. She had a record, now. She was a criminal, just like they were. Just a number in a system that had no reason to do anything but lock her away, and shut her up.

Consuelo closed her eyes and rolled on her side facing the wall. She willed herself to sleep, but that welcome escape wouldn't come.

CHAPTER SEVEN

ROSARIO

The package from Amazon arrived a few days after Rosario's talk with Lei, just after the morning breakfast rush. Rosario wiped her hands on her apron and took the box from the deliveryman. She carried it straight back into the tiny office behind the kitchen, where Momi was sorting the morning's meal tickets and whizzing through the accounting on her old-fashioned adding machine.

Rosario took a moment in the doorway to gaze at her dear friend. The late morning sun came through a small window up above her partner's desk and shone down on the beautiful, thick mass of Momi's long black hair, just beginning to glitter with silver. Momi danced hula in a well-known *halau*, and she kept her hair and skin shiny and healthy with coconut oil.

Rosario had *feelings* for Momi. Sometimes she hoped that the other woman had feelings for her too, but they had never spoken of them or acted on them.

Her friend looked up from the pile of receipts. "Come in, Rosie. Take a load off and put your feet up. You been working too hard, as usual." She pushed a stool out from under her desk and set it in front of the old armchair beside her desk.

Rosario sat in the chair and elevated her feet, sighing with pleasure to take the weight off swollen ankles. She handed Momi the package. "Lei ordered these special cameras. They're supposed to hook up to my smartphone. Let's put one outside the walk-in, and another one in here, since you told me there were crumbs."

Momi nodded. "Sounds good. It still seems like someone has been coming in here, but I can't quite put my finger on what's different, other than the crumbs."

"Then let's get to it, and put up these cameras. I'm ready to catch our burglar in the act."

THAT EVENING, when Rosario walked the six blocks from the restaurant to her little 1920s bungalow on D Street, she enjoyed the crispness of approaching California winter.

People were already hanging their lights and putting out their decorations. Now that she knew Lei was coming, and hopefully bringing a young friend, it would be worth it to dig out the old wooden nativity set that Lei used to love to play with when she was a girl, and have her neighbor help her put lights up around the house.

Rosario's heart was heavy as she missed Lei's father, her brother Wayne, still in a post-jail rehab setting. In spite of his record, Wayne was a good man. He'd tried to take the easy way in life and that led him down the wrong path, but he'd become a Christian in prison, kicked all drugs, and it seemed like he had really turned over a new page in his life.

Hopefully Wayne would want to help her in the restaurant when he got out of his program. He had always been just as good a cook as she was, and she could really use the help in the kitchen. With Wayne working there too, she might even get a day off once in a while.

Rosario had barely unlocked the front door of her house when her phone dinged.

She glanced down at the app that was connected to the restaurant's brand-new surveillance nanny-cams. It pulsed red at her.

Rosario dropped her handbag just inside the front door and hastily locked it.

The phone beacon was alarming, and nervousness made her mouth go dry. She was almost afraid to see who was going into her fridge.

"Does it really matter?" she said aloud. *But it did.* Someone was taking food behind her back, and it had to stop.

She hit the app's button, and a camera window opened up.

Visibility was dim around the door of the fridge, but she immediately recognized the tall, gangly, bushy-headed outline of Josef.

"Oh no!" Rosario covered her mouth with her hand. Her favorite young busboy and helper opened the door of the walk-in and held it wide, propping it open with a stool. "Oh my goodness, that's why the electric bill has been going up so much!" she muttered. "Josef, I can't believe it's you!"

Her breathing tight with sadness and anger, she watched as Josef turned and gestured. With a start, Rosario realized that the office icon was also lit up. She hit the button to open a second camera window beside the first, and gasped at the sight of two children tugging flour sacks off the stack and onto the floor of Momi's office. The dim security lights that they left on inside the building lit up a young girl, and an even younger boy.

Josef was clearly in charge. He came out of the refrigerator with his arms filled with food and the younger children met him as he returned.

Rosario swallowed a lump in her throat—the things they carried were the small pail of hard-boiled eggs that hadn't sold at the counter, expired sandwich bread, a vat of peanut butter, and the overripe mangoes and pineapple cores from the plastic pig slop bin.

These kids must be starving. *What had happened to their parents?*

Josef was clearly careful not to take the good food that she needed to run the restaurant. Tears filled her eyes as the three children sat down on the floor in Momi's office, and Josef made them peanut butter and mango sandwiches while the younger children gorged themselves on hard-boiled eggs.

When they had eaten their fill, Josef took all the remaining food back into the walk-in, closed the door and replaced the stool. The three of them walked into the office, and two of the kids arranged sacks on the floor. The children pulled the empty coffee and flour sacks over themselves, curled up, and went to sleep.

Rosario closed the surveillance windows on her app.

She had an answer as to what was going on inside the restaurant.

Clearly these children had somehow lost their parents. She tried to remember what Josef had told her about his family, but he had been evasive. She'd seen his high school ID card and it had been enough to verify his age to hire him—but she hadn't known he was *homeless!* And he was taking care of a younger brother and sister.

She had to come up with something better for them, something that didn't get them separated in foster care, or worse yet, deported from the United States without anyone to care for them.

Rosario clenched her jaw.

She would take care of Josef and his brother and sister. God hadn't given her so much love and so many resources and no children of her own for all of her many blessings not to be shared.

Her mind was made up.

She turned briskly to walk into her own kitchen. She had some calls to make, and some beds to make up, and she was energized to do what needed to be done.

But still, it hurt that Josef hadn't trusted her enough to ask for help. Made her eyes prickle to think of it. *Poor boy.* Carrying so much weight, all alone. Somehow, she had to convince him to trust her.

She'd prove to them she had plenty of room—in her heart, and in her home. Bringing Lei home at nine had already shown her that. Those children wouldn't have to spend one more night sleeping in Momi's office on sacks of rice and flour if she could help it.

CHAPTER EIGHT

CONSUELO

Days seemed to have passed in the dim half-light that was the perpetual state of things in the 'shoe.' Consuelo tossed to and fro on her pallet. Her mind wouldn't stop going over the series of events that had led to now: that glorious day she'd stolen an airplane, and grabbed up Angel on impulse, beginning a terrifying and exhilarating crime spree of robbing the rich and giving to the poor.

That exciting adventure had ended so badly. So many had been hurt. But she couldn't take responsibility for where it had gone. She'd never intended any of what the Smiley Bandit movement had unleashed—but it was clear now that, yes, *she needed to tell her story* . . . or it would be permanently twisted into what others interpreted, and the media had promoted.

She finally slept.

Hours or only minutes might have passed when Consuelo heard the metallic grind of the door unlocking, and it opened.

Consuelo sat up. Aunty Marcie's face was impassive. "You have a visitor."

"I thought I couldn't have visitors." Consuelo's voice was a thin rasp.

"Your lawyer is not considered a visitor," Aunty Marcie said.

"Thank God." Consuelo stood, her legs a little wobbly, and preceded the CO down the hall. Marcie put her in a bare conference room with a battered table, rather than the usual group visiting area. Consuelo sat on one of the molded plastic chairs.

Bennie Fernandez, his white hair standing up in a halo, wasn't the only visitor. Lei Texeira, her eyes worried, followed him in, and right behind them, bright as a parakeet in a teal-green pantsuit, was Wendy Watanabe. Bringing up the rear of their little parade, was a *haole* man that Consuelo recognized as the warden.

"I'm so glad to see you," Consuelo told Lei. "Thank you for coming." She had to blink—her eyes were stinging. Lei sat next to her and touched her arm lightly—she wasn't much for hugging.

Not so Wendy. "Oh, my God, girl. What did they do to you?" The petite reporter exclaimed, swooping in to engulf Consuelo in a waft of *pikake* perfume and strong, toned arms.

"The inmate was captured breaching the wall in an attempt to escape off of the property," the warden harrumphed. "She's in the isolation unit, standard intervention after a runaway attempt."

"No, sir, I didn't want to escape." Consuelo extricated herself from Wendy's grip. "I was fighting to get away from the other girls. I left a note under my mattress asking for help."

"That's why Warden Smith allowed this meeting." Fernandez tugged his aloha shirt down over his paunch. "One of the COs, Marcie Porter, found it in your cell."

"I was hoping someone would find the note, and know that I didn't participate willingly," Consuelo said.

Warden Smith's face looked thunderously angry. He'd happily keep her in the isolation unit indefinitely, she was sure of it. She had to hurry and say what she needed to in front of witnesses before he found a way to do that. "I have information. About Fai's uncle. He has contacts here in the prison, and he helped her escape. He's a member of the Boyz."

"Jose Taika," Lei said. "I ran background on your roommate Fai already. She's well-connected with organized crime."

Smith's eyebrows drew together. "Well. We didn't have that information. If we had, I might have taken your concerns more seriously, Special Agent Texeira."

Lei cocked a brow skeptically. "I've already called a contact at HPD that I'd like to have help with the hunt for the missing girls. I just came to verify that Consuelo was unhurt, and to see if she had any more information for us?"

"Yes, I do." Consuelo swallowed. "But I'm afraid. Of what could happen. From Fai and her relatives."

"I am requesting a change of location for you because of this incident," Bennie Fernandez said. "I'm going straight to the judge who worked your case. And I'm sure Warden Smith plans different accommodations for you in light of all of this?"

Warden Smith opened his mouth. "Well . . ." he stammered, his face empurpled. "We can't make exceptions. Aguilar has a sentence to fulfill."

Wendy whipped a small recorder out of her pocket and turned it on, extending the device toward Smith while speaking into a mic she'd slipped onto her head. "This is Wendy Watanabe with KHIN-2 news. I'm here with Warden Smith of Oahu Youth Correctional Facility, doing a follow-up story about Consuelo Aguilar. This notorious folk heroine was recently involved with a breakout, and is now cooperating with authorities in the capture of the escapees. Warden Smith, what can you tell us about how the facility plans to assist in the capture of the runaways?"

"Ah. Yes." Smith smoothed his tie over his shirt and sucked in his belly. "Every resource will be deployed to assist in the capture of the criminals at large."

"And what is being done to protect Aguilar, a critical witness in this case?" Watanabe was relentless as she held the microphone of the recorder close to Smith's sweating face.

"We'll—move her to a protected isolation unit," Smith said. "We appreciate law enforcement's prompt, coordinated effort in recovering the escapees."

"You heard it here first, folks. Every resource deployed and Aguilar will be protected." Watanabe clicked *Off* on the recorder and smiled, a twitch of shapely scarlet lips. "Thrilled to hear it, Warden Smith."

Lei made a shooing motion with her hand. "Mr. Fernandez and I need to speak to Consuelo alone regarding an active case and her sensitive information—not to mention her future testimony. Can the rest of you wait outside?"

Consuelo's heart rate was still galloping as Wendy Watanabe and Warden Smith filed out. "Please. Get me a notebook," she whispered. "I need to write while I'm in isolation."

"Way ahead of you, girl." Lei drew Consuelo's precious notebook out of her backpack, along with a plain Bic ballpoint. "The pen sucks, but it passed regulations."

Consuelo clasped the notebook to her chest. "Thanks so much."

"You're welcome. Now tell me everything."

Consuelo did: all she knew about Fai, her relatives, the escape plan, and their rendezvous point if separated.

She felt much lighter as she was led back to the isolation unit half an hour later, the notebook concealed under her shirt.

CHAPTER NINE

LEI

Lei strode out of the youth facility, Bennie Fernandez trotting in her wake. "Like we discussed, I'm filing for a change of venue to move Consuelo to a therapeutic correctional group home for girls in California," Bennie puffed. "It's a lot homier than this place."

"Great, Bennie. You've done good by her. But don't let me hear of you defending any of these scumbags," Lei admonished, shaking a finger at him. "I'll cite conflict of interest on you in a heartbeat."

"All's fair," the defense lawyer said as they reached the parking lot. "In love, and in defense law. But don't worry. I checked with my office. No Taikas or Afas on the client list."

"Keep it that way." Lei raised a hand to him as he got into a boat-sized Lincoln Continental.

Lei beeped open her truck and jumped in, peeling out of the lot. She put her cop light on and picked up her radio, checking in with Marcus Kamuela, the detective in charge of the OYCF's manhunt.

"Got some new information from a witness," she told the big Hawaiian detective. "Let's rendezvous in five minutes."

She met Kamuela and the other HPD operatives at the Kaneohe police station. There, she shared the intel Consuelo had gathered—the name of the warehouse where the fugitives were meeting with a contact to move them even further away. "A boat is involved," Lei said. "That's all my witness knew."

"We need the Coast Guard in on this," Kamuela said. "And SWAT. I'm making the calls. It's on—we're going to nail these Boyz."

THE MULTI-AGENCY GROUP of law enforcement personnel approached a rusty steel warehouse located at one end of the harbor area. The industrial zone of grubby older buildings draped in power lines was an urban blight that contrasted with sparkling turquoise ocean in the distance.

Lei stayed well back, remembering her 'consultant' role, as SWAT burst in the warehouse entrance with a handheld metal door cannon. There was a mad scramble inside the warehouse, the rattle of gunfire, and a burst of yelling. The roar of engines added further chaos, and a twin-engine speedboat zoomed out of the side of the warehouse butted up against the water.

Lei hadn't entered with the team, and she ran along the outside of the building, her weapon in low ready position, tracking the fleeing boat.

Driving the boat was a suspect in a ball cap. Staring back at the shore from the craft, their faces pale with fright, were a heavyset girl with black hair and a slim blonde. And in the stern, raising a shotgun to fire at Lei, was another male suspect.

Lei ducked as a hole blew open in the corrugated metal wall near her with a noise like the world was ending. She swung back around and fired, aiming for the big twin Mercury engines. Fai Afa gave a cry and jumped back, grabbing the blonde Jadene in her arms as they dodged a ricochet off the motor's protective shell. The man with the shotgun hit Lei's shed again.

Lei fired back, still going for the engine, and this time the motor seemed to stutter—but the speedboat kept going, slamming into waves and bouncing high, a tough target to hit on a wide-open sea.

Lei didn't want to hit one of the girls. She was already out of range for anything but a wild card shot, so she kept an eye on the boat as Kamuela arrived beside her, panting with exertion. "Interior's secure. Looks like the girls got away."

"How far out is that Coast Guard cutter?" Lei asked. "I did get off a couple of shots. Tried to hit the motor. Seemed like I did, but it's still moving."

As if in answer to her question, they saw the smaller of the Coast Guard's intercept boats moving in on the speedboat, which had slowed a bit.

"Maybe I winged it," Lei muttered, sheltering her eyes with a hand against the glitter of sunshine on the ocean.

"I think you did." Marcus lifted his rifle in burly arms and peered through its scope at the distant, bobbing boats. "Looks like the Coast Guard's superior firepower has intimidated them. They're taking the craft in tow." The big Hawaiian's stern face split in a grin as he high-fived Lei. "Tell your girl Consuelo she did nice work. We scooped up some major players in the Boyz today, thanks to her."

"I'll make sure she gets that message," Lei said. "We're moving her somewhere safer to make sure she's out of their range."

"Good idea. And just in time for Christmas," Marcus said, as they turned back to meet with their team and process the captives they'd taken inside the warehouse.

"Her lawyer's working on a new placement, and if all goes well, she'll be moved before the holiday." Lei held up her hand. "Fingers crossed."

Marcus laughed. "With you and that reporter following her case, I wouldn't be at all surprised if Consuelo gets that publishing deal everybody's talking about, and ends up going to college."

"That's my hope," Lei said. "Consuelo deserves a break, and she can do better for the world telling her story and fulfilling an education than sitting in a jail cell. I just hope the powers that be agree with Wendy, Bennie and me on that score."

CHAPTER TEN

ROSARIO

Rosario rose early the next morning, dressing quickly. She wanted to intercept Josef before the children left; she suspected he got up and began his work shift for her at four thirty a.m., and probably let the younger ones sleep in.

She took the car this morning to shave time off her trip, parking it a block away from the restaurant so as not to spook her visitors.

She checked on the app to see that the children were still sleeping on their makeshift beds in Momi's office. She wasn't surprised, however, when the app alerted her to movement outside the walk-in—Josef was bringing out the cold rice she'd made the previous evening to press it into blocks for musubi. Her heart seemed to give a little lurch and squeeze as she watched the gangly teen set up in the kitchen, carefully laying out all the ingredients for the musubi on the work counter, including a big roll of industrial-grade plastic wrap.

She couldn't be angry with him. Josef was working hard, just trying to survive and provide for and protect his young siblings.

She went to the back door and inserted the key quietly, deactivating the alarm with her code before it could even beep. Then she shut the door soundlessly behind her, and tiptoed through the storage area, past Momi's office closed door, and into the kitchen.

"Good morning, Josef," she said, reaching for her apron which was hanging from its hook on the back of the door into the main restaurant area.

Josef started and spun toward her, his eyes going wide with fright. He was wearing earbuds, which had masked her approach. "Aunty!" He exclaimed in a loud whisper, his eyes glancing toward Momi's closed office door. "What are you doing here so early?"

Rosario tied on her apron. "I remembered I had to throw out all the hard-boiled eggs from yesterday and that there wouldn't be any for the front counter. I thought I'd come in early, get that done, help you, and we could get an early start on the day."

"Okay," Josef said. He had begun scooping rice into a press where it was compacted into rectangular blocks.

Rosario moved to stand between him and the office door. The kids probably had some escape plan for if they were ever discovered, and it probably involved climbing out through the window above Momi's desk. She didn't want to spook them into flight. She'd be just sick if they all ran away and she couldn't help them. Keeping her voice low, Rosario took down the big pot she cooked the eggs in. "I know what's going on, Josef, and I want to help."

The boy hid behind the bushy growth of his hair, ducking his head further, his gloved hands moving like lightning as he scooped, pressed, and stacked the blocks of rice. "I don't know what you mean, Aunty."

"Your brother and sister. Sleeping in Momi's office."

Josef's head flew up like a startled deer. "We never meant no harm."

"I know that. And I want to help you."

But Josef was backing away, the metal rice scoop held up in front of him like a sword as he tried to angle around her toward the office door. "Please don't turn us in. They'll put us in cages at the border. Separate us . . ."

"I know, Josef, I know, and I'm so sorry for whatever's happened to make you have to do this. Live like this." Rosario held out her hands to try to cut him off from making a dash to the door, alerting his siblings. "Please. Sit down with me. Let me fix us a cup of hot chocolate and talk things over. I have an idea I'd like to run by you." She slowly closed her arms and made prayer hands, letting her emotion show in her eyes as she pleaded with him. "Please, Josef. Have I ever done anything to hurt you?"

The boy slowly lowered the metal spoon. "No, Aunty. You've been so good to me."

"Well then. Trust me a little, won't you?" She let a little of her hurt creep into her voice as she took a couple of big china mugs off the rack and held them under the instant hot water tap, filling them with piping-hot water. "You know where the chocolate is. And get us a couple of marshmallows, too."

Josef cocked his head, eyeing her from beneath the floppy black bangs on his forehead. Rosario paid no mind, opening a nearby drawer for a pair of spoons, but she let out a breath of relief when he turned and went to the dry goods storage cabinet, bringing down a canister of excellent quality chocolate she saved for special desserts—and moments like these. He grabbed the bag of marshmallows as well.

"Go sit down at my little table." She pointed.

Right next to the swinging doors that separated the kitchen from the restaurant's dining room was a small square table covered in oilcloth and stacked with restaurant supply catalogs. Whenever she wasn't cooking or in Momi's office, Rosario could be found there, keeping an eye on the dining room and resting her feet on a footstool under the table. A second folding chair leaned against the wall, for when she had to talk to an employee for some reason.

She and Josef had already had several sit-downs at her "conference table," as the staff called her special spot.

Rosario heaped their cups with a generous portion of cocoa, stirred it in, and decorated the tops with marshmallows. She carried the mugs over to the table. Josef was already seated on the folding chair, his long legs extended but flexed, as if at any moment he would jump up and run.

And he might still do just that.

She pushed a mug over to him, along with a spoon. "I like to let mine sit for a few minutes. Let it cool a bit, let the marshmallows melt." She stirred hers gently.

Josef made no move to take the cocoa. "How can you help us?"

"You and your brother and sister can come live with me. We don't say anything to anyone unless we have to." Rosario blew on her cocoa, and took a careful sip. "You are already known here as my busboy, someone I regard as a *hanai* son. If we have to, we will tell people that you children are staying with me for a while, since your parents are working out of town."

"What is *hanai*?"

"In Hawaii, *hanai* is an informal form of adoption. We can 'adopt' a child of a friend or relative and it becomes as if they were blood."

Josef's eyes dropped and his lower lip trembled. He picked up his spoon and tentatively stirred his cocoa. "You think of me that way? As a son?"

"I do," Rosario said steadily. "Where are your parents, Josef?"

"They're dead."

She had suspected that might be the case, but the flatness and finality with which he said the words made her clutch her heart. "*Auwe!* I'm so sorry."

Josef kept his eyes down. He took a sip of cocoa. "They were killed by a drug gang."

"Why?"

"My father carried drugs across the border for one of the cartels. He did it to pay for Mama and us kids to get passage into the United States. Then he got caught by a rival gang. They made an example out of him and Mama. At least, that's what I think happened. That's what the newspaper said."

"Oh no." Rosario covered her mouth with a hand. "How did you escape?"

"We had a secret place under the house they had made for us if we had to hide. I was here at the restaurant, working, when it happened. My brother and sister hid when the men came to the house. When I came home from work, I found them." Josef still wouldn't look at her, but now his hand was shaking so badly the cocoa spilled out onto the tablecloth. "I got Isabella and Carlos out of the house. I didn't let them see anything, what happened to our parents. But since then, we have been going to school during the day, and then hiding here after dark." He sipped his hot chocolate, and the cup rattled against his teeth. "I didn't know where else to go, what I could do to take care of them."

"Why didn't you tell me? Let me help you sooner?" Rosario reached over and caught his hand in one of hers. "Surely you knew I would help you."

"I couldn't take the chance," Josef said woodenly. "My brother and sister—all we have is each other. Our family is gone in Mexico. All from the cartels."

"You're hiding from them?"

Josef nodded. "I was afraid to go to anyone. They could find us. And if it was immigration, we would be separated. Deported . . ." Fear widened his eyes. "You won't turn us in? Or kick us out? You promise?"

"Josef." Rosario patted the back of the boy's hand as she held it. She wished she could hug him, but he was too afraid, too trau-matized. *Maybe someday.* "You are going to find out what *'ohana'* means in Hawaiian culture. We care for our own. You and your brother and sister are family now." She stood up. "Take me in and introduce me."

"Yes, Aunty." He stood, and led her to the door of the office.

"How did you get in?" she whispered, pointing to the door's keyhole.

Josef ducked his head in shame. "I made a copy of Aunty Momi's key. I'm sorry. But we never took anything except things you were already throwing away."

"I know." Rosario laid a hand on his slender shoulder, unable to keep from touching him. "It's okay."

Josef opened the door, and turned on the lamp on the desk.

Immediately the children sat up.

Rosario stifled a gasp—*they were so adorable!* They both had Josef's large, brown, long-lashed eyes. The little boy's hair was a tangled mass of curls, the girl's fell down her back in a thick black braid. They'd only taken off their shoes and were still wearing street clothes that looked like they'd been worn for days. Covered by flour sacks, they looked like what they were—beautiful, sweet, scared orphans in need of love, food, and a clean home.

Her heart melted as she smiled. "Aloha, *keiki*. That means 'hello, children.'"

Clearly terrified, the two huddled together, darting glances between Josef, Rosario, and the door.

Josef smiled. "It's okay." He gestured to Rosario. "*Esta Tante Rosario*. She help us."

Rosario squatted down to their level, wincing at her arthritic knees. "You kids like hot chocolate?" Slowly, hesitantly, the *keiki* nodded.

Soon she'd fed them all breakfast made on the big grill. She drove them back to the house for showers, and showed them the bedrooms she'd made up for them.

All three were silent but compliant, cleaning up and allowing her to wash all of their dirty clothes. Once she had the clothes in the washer, she breathed a little easier. *They couldn't run away with all they owned in her washing machine!*

Once the children were clean and dressed, she handed each of them a brown bag lunch of neatly packed restaurant leftovers.

"Your clothes will be clean and dry when you get home from school." She shook a finger at Josef. "The key is under the rock by the back door. And I expect you at the restaurant this afternoon at the usual time."

She watched the three of them walk down the street toward their schools.

She could only hope they'd be here when she got home from the restaurant—and she already cared too much that they would be.

CHAPTER ELEVEN

***CONSUELO** — several weeks later*

Consuelo took a shuttle from the San Francisco airport to San Rafael with Lei, who had been appointed her temporary guardian *ad litem*, an advocacy role used in orphan cases by the Hawaii courts. They then took a rideshare from the bus stop to her aunt's little house on D Street. "Aunty couldn't get us because she's at work at the restaurant," Lei had explained to Consuelo. She had spent a bit of their plane flight from Honolulu telling Consuelo more of her story, and why Rosario was the closest thing Lei had to a mother. "She has a big heart. She's taken in three kids who would have been deported. They are all living at the house with her now. She says it's going great."

"They were lucky that your aunt was so understanding," Consuelo said, fiddling with her ever present notebook.

"You're right about that," Lei said. "Aunty is really something. I think you'll like her."

Lei located the house key, hiding under a rock like it had been for years, and unlocked the side door.

The little three-bedroom bungalow felt cozy and smelled of ginger and cinnamon from a big bowl of potpourri on the round kitchen table. Lights strung around the living room and a brightly decorated Christmas tree added to the festive feeling.

Consuelo glanced around the tidy house, filled with Hawaiiana decor. Nineteen forties-era *koa* wood furniture dressed in Hawaiian print slipcovers filled the living room. A lamp in the shape of a pineapple decorated a side table. The kitchen was bright with tile squares painted with palm trees and tropical fruit. They headed through the house, and Lei pointed in through a doorway to a small bedroom, crowded with a set of bunk beds and a single twin separated by a tall chest of drawers. Clothing and backpacks hung neatly on hooks on the wall. "That used to be my room. Aunty said she offered to split up the kids so the boys, Josef and Carlos, could be in one room and the girl, Isabella, in another, but they wanted to all stay together."

Consuelo could easily imagine that, after what she'd heard had happened to them. Consuelo and Lei dropped their bags on the two twin beds in the guestroom.

"I love this house," Consuelo said. "It feels like being in Hawaii, even though we're in California."

Lei smiled. "It was a refuge for me, too, when Aunty took me in. I was about Isabella's age. I have a little bit of an idea of what they are going through."

"So do I," said Consuelo, peering in at the bunk beds. "Only I didn't have any brothers or sisters. It might have been easier if I had."

Lei pulled her in for a brief hug. "They say what doesn't kill you makes you stronger. We must be really, really strong."

"I guess we are." Consuelo smiled. Her face felt stiff, like she hadn't done that in a while.

They walked the six blocks to the restaurant through the yellow, orange and brown leaves that blew along the sidewalk, and Consuelo slid her hands into the pockets of her jeans and hunched her shoulders in her thin parka.

She glanced at Lei. Her guardian's curly hair was the color of the fall leaves, all of those dark, warm tones, matched by the smatter of freckles across her nose and set off by her big smile. Lei was better than pretty to look at—she was *interesting*.

"It's going to get colder than this here in California. I'll make sure the folks at the group home get you some warmer clothes." Lei said. "Are you worried about the new setting?"

The place Consuelo was transferring to after their holidays together was only an hour away, in a town called Walnut Creek. Consuelo had seen the brochure; it looked pleasant enough. "Anything is better than 'the shoe' at OYCF."

Lei shook her head. "I have to agree with you there."

They reached the restaurant, a nice but unpretentious-looking storefront in a strip mall, with a sign trimmed in neon spelling out *Aunty's Hawaiian Food Place*.

The back door was unlocked and tinkled as Lei opened it. Consuelo followed her into a solid wall of delicious smells. She inhaled deeply, and Lei turned to her with a sparkle in her eyes. "Aunty has been cooking for days to get ready for this dinner."

"The restaurant isn't normally open on Christmas Eve?"

"Just once during the day, which we are preparing for. Aunty opens it to do a big meal for the homeless, a free Christmas dinner for anyone in need. And when you to get to know Aunty, you'll realize that she never does anything halfway."

Consuelo followed Lei through a cluttered storage area, and into the kitchen.

A short, plump older woman, wrapped in a large plumeria print apron, was wielding a spatula to toss sweet onions, macadamia nuts, and water chestnuts on a huge iron grill. Her warm brown skin gleamed with perspiration. Salt-and-pepper curls sprang from underneath a chef's hat, to surround her smiling face. "*Aloha*, Lei! You here at last!"

"We got here as fast as we could." Lei embraced her aunt.

"Well, you two got here just in time to help me with the final prep. Not that I don't have plenty of helpers." A dimple appeared in Rosario's cheek that mirrored the one Consuelo had noticed in Lei's cheek, too. "This must be your friend Consuelo." Rosario wiped her hands on her apron, and held one of them out. *"Welina 'ia kā mākou home a me ko mākou ohana."* Welcome to our home and family.

The sound of Hawaiian language being spoken, and such a warm greeting, brought tears prickling to Consuelo's eyes—and she couldn't remember when she had last cried. "Mahalo, Aunty," she whispered.

Rosario pulled her into a hug. "You are welcome here. *E komo mai.*"

Consuelo let herself rest a moment against Aunty's well-padded shoulder. She could imagine what it might've been like to have someone like Rosario take her in when her mother was hit by a car, when her father passed away from cancer.

Her life might've been a whole lot different.

But at least she had *now,* and now was pretty wonderful.

"You can help Josef set up the tables out in the dining room with the kids." Aunty turned and hollered out through the swinging doors. "Keiki! Come meet my niece and her friend!"

The swinging doors opened and three young people appeared, wearing the restaurant's trademark plumeria print aprons and felt reindeer headdresses that sparkled with LED lights. One was a tall boy with hair so newly shorn that pale skin showed around his ears against his brown complexion. A girl about ten years old smiled and waved, and their little brother held out a felt reindeer headband covered with lights. "For you. *Feliz Navidad.*"

Consuelo smiled and pressed the little button on the back of the headband. The festive decoration lit up in a blinking pattern, and she put the antlers on her head. *"Hola. Me llamo Consuelo."*

The little girl burst into a spate of Spanish. The kids clearly thought that she, too, was Mexican. Consuelo held her hands up, waving them in a signal to slow down. *"Mi Español no está muy bien. Solo aprendí en la escuela. Yo soy Filipina, from Hawaii."*

"We are very happy to meet you," Josef's gaze was admiring. "Aunty said you would help us with the setting and table decorations?"

Consuelo glanced back at Lei. "Sure. Whatever you need."

Her guardian's grin was huge. "You kids look so festive. Go on. I'll help Aunty in the kitchen."

Consuelo's three new friends surrounded her, and she went out through the swinging doors to help set up a room filled with Christmas music, lights, and pretty decorations.

CHAPTER TWELVE

LEI

Lei watched her ward go out into the dining room, and turned back to Rosario. "Oh, Aunty, it's so good to see you." They embraced again. Lei was only five foot six, but she was still tall enough to rest her cheek against Aunty's head. "You're doing a good thing with those kids."

"Glad my FBI niece approves." Rosario patted Lei's arm. "Nuff of this. We have a Christmas dinner to get on!"

An hour later, Lei and Consuelo unlocked and opened the main doors of the restaurant. The homeless folks they'd invited through various social service agencies and by posting flyers around town were waiting outside. The people quickly filled all of the seats in the restaurant, and a buffet line formed with Rosario and the kids dishing up the delicious Hawaiian feast of *kalua* pork, *laulau*, *lomi* salmon, *poke*, *limu* and regular salad, *poi*, rice and a whole table of Hawaiian style desserts. Lei, Consuelo, Momi and her family waited on the large group, wielding pitchers of water, eggnog, coffee and tea. And when each person left, they carried a bag of leftovers and a red fleece stocking, filled with treats and hygiene supplies donated by a local charity.

Finally, all the serving and clearing were done. Momi and Rosario pushed several tables together so that everyone who'd helped could heap their plates and sit down to eat the remainder of the holiday feast. Hawaiian style Christmas carols played loudly in the background as they exchanged simple gifts.

After they'd eaten, Lei leaned her chair on its back legs and rubbed her tummy, emitting a little burp. "So *ono*, Aunty. This is a good thing you're doing for the community."

Rosario patted Momi's shoulder. "We do what we can."

"And we love what we do," Momi finished.

"That's why we have a present for you," Josef said. He tilted his head at the younger kids, and Isabella and Carlos ran into the back. Lei heard the sound of the walk-in fridge opening, and her brows went up in surprise as she exchanged a glance with her aunt.

Rosario turned to Momi. "You know what they're up to?"

"Nope." Momi shook her head, bouncing her youngest grand-daughter on her knee. A widow, her two grown children had brought their spouses and kids to help out and enjoy the Christmas feast as well.

Moments later the two children came back in, carrying a loosely wrapped, festive-looking cardboard box. "We made this for you two Aunties," Isabella said shyly.

"Hope you like it," Carlos said, clasping his hands with excitement. "Open it!"

Two red spots appeared on Aunty's cheeks as she took hold of the lid of the box, lifting it off. She peered inside. "Oh, my goodness."

"Here, turn on the light," Josef said, pressing a cord that extruded from the back of the box. A star nightlight bloomed on the inside of the box, illuminating a nativity scene inside made of colored, claylike substance.

"It's marzipan," Carlos said. "You can eat it!" He reached inside and plucked a "pumpkin" from inside the miniature stable, and held it out to Rosario. "Try it, Aunty!"

Rosario opened her mouth, and Carlos popped the object in. Everyone waited while she chewed thoughtfully, her eyes closed. "Delicious!" she pronounced. "This is just wonderful! Look at baby Jesus in his manger, and you even have a donkey!"

"The camel was the hardest," Isabella said. "We did a one-humped camel because the other kind was even more hard."

"The dromedary was even more difficult," Josef corrected, very much the big brother making sure her grammar was correct. Everyone was persuaded to try a bit of the marzipan, and Lei liked the nut paste's unique flavor. She squinted at the lumpy camel held up by pipe cleaner legs. "So creative. I can totally tell what it is."

"I love it," Aunty Rosario said. "Come give me a hug, kids. We'll keep it forever."

"You're supposed to eat it!" Carlos protested.

Aunty shook her head. "No. It's too special." And she carried the box with its manger scene and set it right in the window of the restaurant for all to see.

CHAPTER THIRTEEN

Lei

Lei drove Consuelo to her new placement at Walnut Creek two days after Christmas, navigating through heavy Bay Area traffic and onto a giant freeway. The two of them were silent in the rental car, each lost in her thoughts, as an hour or so later, they approached the community tucked into a valley among hills covered in golden grass and deep green live oaks.

Lei could still feel Aunty Rosario's arms around her in the longest hug as they'd said goodbye that morning. Her aunt had taken on a lot with those kids, and Lei wanted to worry about the extra work and strain on Rosario—but it was obvious that the benefits outweighed the costs for her bighearted aunt. Rosario was energized by having "the keiki" to care for, a buzzing bee of energy as she gathered supplies for them and sought out a lawyer and a social service agency whose advocacy she could trust in getting longer-term custody of the children.

Meanwhile, Josef, Isabella and Carlos were clearly blooming under her care, helping with the house and yard, and becoming more open and affectionate by the day. Josef was on his way to being her right-hand man at the restaurant. They were even talking about getting a dog.

"I wish we could have had longer with Aunty and her new family." Lei finally broke their companionable silence to address her ward. "But Keiki and Angel are boarded, and I've taken all the time I can from work."

"I know. It's fine," Consuelo said. She was engulfed in a stylish Maui Built hoodie Stevens had sent, and Rosario and the kids had given her a new pair of Chucks that looked good with the jeans Lei had bought her. "I'm ready for whatever comes next."

"Great attitude," Lei said. They pulled into the address of the group home—a large, sprawling mansion tucked among spreading oak trees. "Whoa. This is fancy."

"Wow," Consuelo said.

Lei parked in a turnaround in front of the mansion, and they hardly had time to get out of the car when the large front door, decorated by a holly wreath, opened to show a clutch of teenaged girls.

Consuelo tensed, and Lei touched her shoulder. "They look friendly."

All three of the girls were smiling. They did look nice.

The leader of the pack approached, wearing black Goth gear and purple hair. She held up a garland of fabric flowers. "Aloha!" she said. "We heard you're from Hawaii, so we brought you a lei."

"Thanks." Consuelo ducked her head awkwardly so the girl could put the lei around her neck.

"Welcome to Creek House. Come on up and we'll show you around, and to your room."

Consuelo looked back at Lei. "I have to say goodbye."

Lei flapped her hand. "Go on. I'll be visiting you again before you know it."

Consuelo broke away from the girls to hug Lei. "Thank you," she whispered, and then let the girls sweep her into the house.

Lei followed at her own speed, carrying Consuelo's backpack.

She handed it over to the houseparent at the door, checked on all the paperwork, signed various forms, and then, from the driveway, called the cell phone she'd given Consuelo.

"Hey. I thought you left," Consuelo said. "But you're still here." She waved down at Lei from a window overlooking the driveway.

"Wanted to make sure you're okay. Really okay. And that those friendly girls aren't pulling an act."

"I really am." Consuelo said. "I have my notebook. And my own room. The girls really are nice. Thank you for getting me a place here." Her voice trembled. "And for Christmas with your aunty and her fosters. I'll never forget it."

"Me neither. It really was great. Well, you get to keep that phone. Call me anytime," Lei said, smiling up at Consuelo as she sat in the window with the phone against her ear. "You got this, babe."

"I got this. Fly safe, back to Hawaii. And kiss Angel for me."

"You know I will." Lei ended the call, waved one last time, and got in the car to head for the airport, and home.

CHAPTER FOURTEEN

ROSARIO

Rosario peeked into the room where the keiki were sleeping. Just to make sure they weren't having nightmares, or getting cold. Both of those things had happened on their first few nights at her house, and now, after they were asleep, she still poked her head in just to make sure they were all right.

A part of her still worried she'd wake up some morning, and they'd have disappeared.

Josef occupied the twin bed closest to the door. His legs in flannel pajamas and long bare feet sprawled from beneath the denim quilt Rosario had made from Wayne's old cowboy jeans seemingly a lifetime ago. The boy slept on his stomach, his face turned sideways into the pillow, his newly cut hair revealing the tender, vulnerable curve of his ear.

He'd trusted her with a sharp pair of scissors applied to his head only days after she'd taken them in. Her hands tingled with the memory of how satisfying it had been to clip away the crazy dreadlocks that had been forming around the nape of his neck, the floppy, greasy strands hiding his face. He was so handsome now that everyone could see him!

Rosario stepped into the room and gently tugged the comforter down over his bare feet, glancing over at the bunks.

Isabella was on the bottom, curled like a shrimp under a Hawaiian quilt Rosario's mama had made when Rosario was still a girl. Her heart felt like it swelled within her chest as she remembered Mama's work-worn hands sewing that beautiful pineapple pattern by hand.

But precious old things got new life by being loved and used again, and that's how it felt to see the sweet face of a sleeping girl under that quilt again after Lei had outgrown it, way too fast.

On the top bunk, Carlos slept on his back with one hand dangling off the bed. She'd let him pick out new bedding, and he wore a red Spiderman set of pajamas to go with the comforter set he'd picked out in honor of his superhero.

They were safe. Well-fed. Cared-for. Nothing fancy, here with her, but a lot of love and a big *ohana* to call their own.

Rosario closed the door softly, and sent her gaze heavenward for a moment. "Thank you, God, for giving me these precious children to care for."

Walking to her own room, she glanced into the guestroom where Lei and Consuelo had so recently slept. God willing, they'd all be back together again next Christmas.

LEI

Lei pulled into her parking spot, a smile already on her lips. Stevens had texted that he was on Oahu for the weekend to celebrate the holidays with her, and would pick up the dogs from the boarder and meet her at her house.

She got out of the truck, and heard Angel's shrill yap, the perfect counterpoint to Keiki's deep booming bark. "Hold on, girls. I'm almost there."

But before she could stick her key in the lock on the tall wooden gate, it opened.

Stevens stood there, a Santa hat on his head and both of the dogs' leashes in his hand. "Don't bother coming in. We're going to the beach for a late Christmas picnic."

"Pinch me. Am I dreaming right now?" Lei exclaimed.

"Yep. I'm your dream man, baby." He grabbed her up for a huge full body hug and a passionate kiss. The dogs went nuts, barking and lunging with excitement.

Finally, he loosened his arms. Lei slid down his lean, hard-muscled length until her feet hit the ground. "I don't know. I'm awfully tired. Maybe I need more convincing about this picnic plan of yours. I might need a nap first." She wiggled her brows suggestively.

"Ha! I'm wise to your evil plans to have your wicked way with me." He picked up a wicker hamper and the dogs' leashes in one fist, and then scooped her up at the waist, tossing her over his shoulder with the other arm. "Food first. A man needs to keep up his strength."

He carried her, giggling, to the truck and put down the tailgate. He set Lei down, and they helped the dogs in, and secured their leashes to the safety toggle she'd rigged up for them.

The two got into the cab and Lei turned on the truck. "It's so good to see you," she said, her eyes filling unexpectedly. "You just made my already great Christmas perfect."

"Okay. You talked me into it. I guess we can kiss a little more," Stevens murmured, his crystal-blue eyes a sea she could swim in forever.

So, they kissed a little more.

And finally, with the lush clouds in the sky going gold and red, they got on the road for their favorite nearby beach. The sun was just setting over the jetty at Ala Moana Beach Park as they carried the picnic basket out to the half-moon of beach, narrow with high tide.

Stevens had packed a bottle of champagne, a couple of plastic flutes, two giant roast beef sandwiches, and slices of *lilikoi* chiffon cake from Napoleon's, Lei's favorite bakery.

They ate, drank, and watched the sunset on sand still warm from the day. The dogs put their heads down and snoozed as the first stars came out and the last of the day shimmered on the gentle waves. "I feel like I've had two Christmases now, with you here and this wonderful meal," Lei said. "This is the best present you could have given me."

"Mission accomplished," Stevens said. "The first of many more spent together."

Lei had to kiss him again, tugging on the fuzzy pom-pom of the Santa hat.

CONSUELO

Consuelo sat at the desk in her pretty bedroom overlooking the mansion's driveway with her notebook open. Lessons were over, and so was dinner, and now she had the evening to hang out with the other girls in the family room, or read and study by herself.

The luxury and freedom of her new setting, after OYCF, were exhilarating.

But it was time to tell her story.

"It all began with a drunk driver," she wrote. *"Just a guy who'd been laid off, had a few too many beers, and didn't even see my mom when he jumped a curb in his old Pontiac."*

As Consuelo wrote, she felt the pressure of locked-up pain begin to drain away.

Nothing could bring her mother, mowed down beside Consuelo on the sidewalk, back to life.

Nothing could change the fact that her father had died an awful death of cancer.

And nothing could save the people murdered by others in her name after she became the Smiley Bandit.

But Consuelo could tell her story. It would help make things right. Stories could change the world, and maybe hers would too—just a little bit.

There were other kinds of freedom than taking to the air in flight, and for now, they were enough.

Turn the page for a sneak peek of book five of the Paradise Crime Mysteries, *Twisted Vine!*

SNEAK PEEK

TWISTED VINE, PARADISE CRIME MYSTERIES BOOK 5

Ken carried the computer and Lei, the rest of the packaged evidence, as they rose in the elevator of the Prince Kuhio Federal Building to the tenth-floor FBI offices. The door opened on the gracious lobby with its marble floors, leather couch, and fan of Guns & Ammo magazines on the coffee table, a fresh-faced New Agent Trainee behind the bulletproof glass booth. The NAT, Amit Gupta, a clean-cut young Indian man, gave a big grin at the sight of them. "Let me help!" he exclaimed, coming out of the cubicle.

"We got it," Lei said, smiling back. It wasn't that long since she'd been sitting where Amit was, and she still remembered the boredom of answering phones and running background checks, which went with the training period—a period that had been extended especially for her due to some procedural mishaps on a case.

Ken waited, his arms full as she juggled her armload of packages, fumbling for her ID badge. Amit took it from her, swiping it through the lock that opened the steel-cored automatic door leading to Bureau headquarters.

Lei took back her badge. "Thanks, Amit." The NAT nodded

and went back into the booth as Ken and Lei's black athletic shoes squeaked down the hall.

Marcella poked her elegant head out of her office. "Lei, stop a minute. I want you to meet someone."

"Let me drop these off first."

"Sure." Marcella pulled back into her office. Lei noticed the blind was down over the door as she passed, and she frowned. Who could be in there? Marcella sometimes liked to "surprise" her, like the time she'd tried to set Lei up again with Alika Wolcott, whom she'd disastrously dated, at the gym. Lei was still in limbo relationship-wise.

Lei had chosen her career in the FBI and left her boyfriend Michael Stevens behind on Maui. Ever the gentleman rescuer, heartbroken and rebuffed, Stevens had married Anchara Mookjai to help the Thai woman get citizenship. While Stevens and Anchara had tried to make their marriage work, Lei's career choice of the FBI had been rocky.

After they'd worked through the drama of his doomed marriage last year, Stevens had gone back to Maui and she'd buckled down and focused on regaining her credibility at the Bureau while they waited for his wife Anchara's citizenship to come through. They were in touch, but only minimally, as phone calls and Skyping just reminded them both how hard it was to wait to be together. Both of them had plenty to do at work without stirring up emotions.

"Let's use Workroom One," Ken said. "I want to get the case file going, and we can inventory these items before we brief Waxman."

"Okay." They turned into the workroom, a functional space with a locked temporary evidence locker, worktables with bright halogen lights over them, computer stations, and various analysis equipment. Lei was eager to fingerprint the heroin kit and the suicide note, but she'd told Marcella she'd be back. "I'll just be a minute," she said, stowing her armload of evidence in the locker.

"You can leave it unlocked. I still have to inventory it," Ken said, setting down the computer on a table. "I'll take this down to Information Technology in a minute, see how soon Sophie can take a look at it."

"Sounds like a plan. I'll be right back," Lei said. She grabbed a water bottle out of the little fridge and hurried back to Marcella's office. She knocked on the door and gave it a push. It swung inward and bumped into Marcus Kamuela. Wrapped in his arms, looking disheveled and thoroughly kissed, was Marcella.

They sprang apart. "Uh—this is Marcus Kamuela, Lei. My boyfriend."

Lei felt a hollowing under her sternum. "The night marchers walking over her tummy" as her aunty Rosario used to say. Of all the people in the world to be dating her best friend, why did it have to be the detective investigating that nemesis from her past, the Kwon murder? "We've met. Saw each other this morning, in fact. Hi again."

"I didn't realize you were the friend Marcella's always talking about," Kamuela said, looking a little sheepish as he straightened his shirt. "Sorry I was irritated this morning. I hate to miss a case."

"I know how you feel about your cases," Lei said, remembering Kamuela's hard cop face in front of the television cameras on the day Charlie Kwon was murdered. She and Kamuela had had a conversation outside Kwon's apartment a year later about the unsolved case. The murder of her childhood molester still held the potential to ruin her life. Lei pasted a smile on her face. "So this is the mystery detective you've been dating, Marcella. Turns out Marcus and I met when I first got to the Bureau."

"Well." Marcella smoothed escaped bits of hair from what she called the "FBI Twist" back into their pins. "I wanted to be sure Marcus and I were going to . . . you know. Be a thing. Before I introduced you."

"She's commitment phobic," Kamuela said, with that crooked, attractive white grin Lei had noticed more than once.

"Well, happy for you guys," Lei said. "Listen, I'd better get back . . ."

"So when is Stevens coming over? We need to do something together, a double date or something," Marcella said.

"I'm not sure." Lei lifted the water bottle in a little toasting gesture. "I'll let you know. Well, gotta run. Carry on." She pulled the door shut on Marcella's laugh, imagining Kamuela sweeping her friend back into his arms and continuing to mess up her hair with kisses.

It made Lei feel a little sick with loneliness and worry. What if Kamuela ever connected her with the Kwon murder? It would devastate Marcella and drive a wedge between all of them. Lei had confronted the pedophile in his apartment on the day he was shot, dressed in a disguise Marcella had unwittingly given her.

Lei ducked into the unisex bathroom and flipped the lock on the door. She did a nervous pee, washed her hands. Her oval face with its sprinkle of cinnamon freckles reflected pale in the silver metal of the paper towel dispenser as she yanked out a handful of towels, running a little water on them and patting her face.

Lei's full mouth tightened as she remembered Charlie Kwon: her mother's boyfriend, drug pusher, and pedophile. Just when she started to forget about it, his unsolved murder would bubble up with its taint of the past. Charlie Kwon, on his knees in front of her with his eyes shut, saying, "Do what you came to do!"

Sophie Ang sat in her computer bay with three large screens ranged around what she called "the cockpit." The low lighting of the FBI's information-technology floor, the sound-deadening walls and carpet, gave the space a womblike feel—but the cool temperature kept the computers humming and agents alert.

And right now, Sophie was feeling more than alert—she was what she'd heard called "wired in." Time seemed to stop, and she entered a state of total synchronicity between the computers, her brain, and her body. Sophie called it "the zone." If she could have, she'd be plugged directly into the mainframe, but such technology didn't yet exist. She knew it was only a matter of time, and she'd be one of the first to sign up.

Sophie had a mug of strong Thai tea at her elbow, and her long golden-brown fingers flew over the keys as she typed in the latest information on Corby Alexander Hale III direct from the scene, piped to her from Lei and Ken through their secure laptop. The photos Lei had taken, their notes, pictures of the suicide note, porn, and heroin kit all flowed through her fingers into the program she'd built.

She'd named it DAVID. The Data Analysis Victim Information Database was designed to analyze crimes into trend-driven subgroups. Unbound by geography or human bias, DAVID was able to mine law-enforcement databases and use statistical probability to hunt down trends that would be missed any other way— and this time, she was finding a trend with an 80-percent confidence ratio. She could add and take away variables that reconfigured the data based on information as it came in. Nationwide, there was an uptick in suicides. Suicides with inconsistencies. Suicides that weren't really suicides.

Sophie still vividly remembered watching the news report a few weeks ago that had caught her interest—a series of odd suicides in Portland. One of the victims, a woman with chronic depression who'd overdosed on sleeping pills, looked uncannily like Sophie's mother.

When she'd entered all the data and hit Submit, DAVID hummed a long moment, the screen blank.

DAVID didn't produce conclusions. It used a probability algorithm that had taken her almost a year to write to provide a percentage of confidence that a given hypothesis was true or false. She had typed in the code for "suicide," having ruled out accidental death herself because of the note and posed quality of the body.

A window popped open: "30-percent chance suicide."

That made it 70-percent probable that Corby Alexander Hale III had been murdered, or assisted in his suicide by someone else—still technically murder.

Sophie pushed back from her bay and stood up, stretching her arms high above her head, arching her back. She bent back down to lay her palms flat on the plastic chair guard on the floor. Other agents dotted around the room didn't look up; they were used to Sophie's frequent workout breaks.

At five foot nine and a hundred and fifty pounds, Sophie Ang was a tall woman with a rangy build and the long muscles of an athlete. She wore loose black rayon pants and a stretchy white blouse with black rubber-soled athletic shoes, well within Bureau guidelines but an outfit that was all about comfort.

Sophie rolled an exercise ball out from under her desk and lay backward, arching all the way over it to stretch. She picked up and crossed two dumbbells on her chest and began a series of sit-ups. When she'd done a hundred, she put down the weights, turned over on her stomach, rolled the ball down to her feet, and did a hundred push-ups.

It was hard to keep fit at a desk job, but Sophie loved mixed martial arts too much to let sitting all day make her soft. After she joined the FBI and learned combat skills, she discovered the Women's Fight Club at her local gym, and she'd been hooked on the intense sport that was a combination of boxing, wrestling, and martial arts.

As Sophie did the push-ups, her busy brain ticked over this new information on the Hale case—information she knew Special Agent in Charge Waxman wouldn't like. In fact, she still had the DAVID program under wraps. She dreaded the moment she had to tell the SAC she was running her own software on the Bureau servers. Truth was, she'd hoped to get some results before she disclosed how she'd come to them.

Any defense attorney would have a field day with the fact that an untested, unsanctioned computer program had generated results pointing to their client. Which was, in fact, a good reason to keep the program secret for the moment—there wasn't a suspect yet to point to, just a confidence ratio that said the boy's death wasn't suicide.

The suicide note appeared to be in his handwriting, though frustratingly general. The fact that there was a note claiming suicide was consistent with those other odd deaths—she'd started a subfile on them, and so far there were forty-eight. Forty-eight suicides across five states with oddities, inconsistencies, evidence others had been involved—but they all had solid, uncoerced-looking suicide notes.

DAVID thought that constellation of factors was statistically improbable with an 80-percent certainty…

Download *Twisted Vine* and continue reading now!

TURN THE PAGE FOR RECIPES FROM AUNTY'S KITCHEN!

RECIPES FROM AUNTY'S HAWAIIAN FOOD PLACE

SUBMITTED BY PARADISE CRIME READERS, KITCHEN TESTED AND ORGANIZED BY ERIN FINIGAN

Recipe Abbreviations

tsp. = teaspoon

Tbsp. = tablespoon

c. = cup

oz. = ounce

fl. oz. = fluid ounce

pt. = pint

qt. = quart

gal. = gallon

lb. = pound

pkg. = package

°F. = Fahrenheit

SAVORIES

HAWAIIAN BEEF STEW

INGREDIENTS:

2 lb. quality beef (stew beef, chuck, Angus, or better) cut into 1-inch cubes.

1½ c. flour (for dredging beef and thickening the sauce)

Salt and pepper

1-3 Tbsp. canola, vegetable, or olive oil

2-3 cloves garlic

1 large onion

1-2 Tbsp. tomato paste

1 can (14-15 oz.) diced tomatoes, regular or stewed (Low sodium is recommended.)

1 8 oz. can tomato sauce (or fresh)

2-3 c. water or low sodium beef or vegetable broth (or 1 c. of each, adding more water later if needed.)

2 bay leaves

1-2 medium potatoes (depending on whether you are using a turnip)

1 c. sliced carrots

1 c. chopped celery

Fresh parsley for garnish and bright flavor
Optional:
Garlic/onion powder for seasoning/dredging meat
Red pepper/chili flakes (to taste for a bit of added depth)
½ Tbsp. finely chopped shallot
Fresh mushrooms
1 medium turnip
1 tsp. of sugar

STEPS:
(Below are instructions for cooking slow cooker, stovetop and Instant Pot versions.)

For all versions:
1. Put the flour (hold out 3 tablespoons of flour) in a zip-top bag. Add salt and pepper and any other seasoning that you like. (For suggestion, see the optional list above under the Ingredients section.) Shake well to mix. Add meat, a few pieces at a time, shaking bag to coat well. Remove the coated meat from the bag and set aside to rest.

2. Chop the onion into small pieces and chop the garlic fine (and shallot if using it) and set aside.

3. Chop the potatoes, carrots and celery, (and turnip if using it) into bite-size pieces and set aside.

4. Heat a skillet (if using the stovetop option, use a Dutch oven or deep pot) to med-high heat, and then add the oil.

5. Once the oil is heated, add the meat a few pieces at a time. (Don't crowd it and do not turn over till the underside is brown. You are not cooking the meat, just browning it to add a bit of caramelization.)

6. Once the meat is browned on all sides, remove from pan.

7. Add the onions to the pan and decrease the heat to low. When the onions become translucent, add the garlic and stir well. Cook 2-3 minutes.

If you are using a slow cooker:
1. Place the meat, onions and the rest of the ingredients (except the remaining flour and parsley) into the slow cooker.

2. Slow cook on low 7-9 hours (best) or 3-5 hours on high.

Optional:
If, at the end of cooking, you would prefer your sauce thicker, make a roux with the remaining flour and equal amounts of butter, water or oil. Stir in pan over high heat until thick. Remove from heat. Scoop 1 cup of liquid from the stew and add to ½ of the roux, then stir well while heating on low. You can add more roux gradually, but be careful not to add too much. Once you have the consistency you like, add the mixture to the slow cooker and stir well. Cook a few more minutes till your sauce has thickened. You may need to add more pepper/pepper flakes, etc. at this point.

If you are using an Instant Pot:
8. Place the meat, onions and the rest of the ingredients (except the remaining flour and parsley) into the Instant Pot.

9. Select the meat/stew option (35-40 minutes cook time and 10-12 minutes cool-down time, depending on the model).

Optional:
If, at the end of cooking, you would prefer your sauce thicker, make a roux with the remaining flour and equal amounts of butter, water or oil. Stir in pan over high heat until thick. Remove from heat.

Scoop 1 cup of liquid from the stew and add to ½ of the roux, then stir well while heating on low. You can add more roux gradually, but be careful not to add too much. Once you have the consistency you like, add the mixture to the Instant Pot and stir well. Cook a few more minutes till your sauce has thickened. You may need to add more pepper/pepper flakes, etc. at this point.

If you are using the stovetop method:
8. Place all the ingredients except the potatoes (and turnip if used), carrots, celery, flour and parsley into a large deep pot or Dutch oven.

9. Bring to a boil, then, reduce heat to medium-low.

10. Simmer with a cover for 2 hours.

11. After two hours, taste the sauce and adjust the seasonings as needed.

12. Add the remaining vegetables and simmer 20-30 minutes more until the vegetables are done.

Optional:
If, at the end of cooking, you would prefer your sauce thicker, make a roux with the remaining flour and equal amounts of butter, water or oil. Stir in pan over high heat until thick. Remove from heat. Scoop 1 cup of liquid from the stew and add to ½ of the roux, then stir well while heating on low. You can add more roux gradually, but be careful not to add too much. Once you have the consistency you like, add the mixture to the other ingredients in the pot and stir well. Cook a few more minutes till your sauce has thickened. You may need to add more pepper/pepper flakes, etc. at this point.

For all versions:
Serve with fresh chopped parsley as a garnish.

TARO/POI ROLLS

SERVINGS:
18-24 (depending on size)

INGREDIENTS:
1⅓ c. warm water (90-105°)
2½ tsp. yeast (Rapid Rise or traditional)
1 egg
1 c. cooked mashed taro root or 1 c. poi (fresh, frozen-thawed, or reconstituted from powder) (Note: Purple potatoes work, but they must be WELL-cooked: steamed or boiled and allowed to completely drain and dry before being mashed.)
½ c. butter or oil (canola or vegetable)
¾ c. to 1 c. of sugar (or bakeable sugar substitute)
¼ tsp. salt
4 c. flour

Optional:
Butter for brushing tops of buns
Sesame (or other) seeds for decorating tops of buns

Garlic/onion powder for the top or for seasoning dough any way that you choose.

STEPS:
1. Preheat oven to 400°F.

2. Start by blooming the yeast. (Add the yeast to warm water and allow it to become fizzy/bubbly; this should take about 10 minutes.)

3. In a large bowl (a mixer bowl if you want to make the dough using dough hooks, or you can mix it all by hand), add the water/yeast mixture.

4. Whisk the egg to break up the yolk.

5. Add the remaining wet ingredients and stir well.

6. Add dry ingredients except flour and stir well.

7. Add flour 1 cup at a time and mix well. Dough should be sticky. (If it seems dry, you can add a tiny bit of water, but start with less and you can always add more.)

8. Flour a flat surface.

9. Turn dough onto floured surface. Break dough into small pieces (dinner roll size, keeping in mind that they will rise a bit).

10. Place rolls onto a greased (or parchment-lined) baking pan or pizza pan.

11. Cover with oiled Saran Wrap or parchment and put in a warm place to rise. (Rolls should double in size in 30-60 minutes.)

12. Once rolls are doubled in size, remove cover, brush with butter and season (if desired).

13. Bake 20 minutes at 400°F.

HAWAIIAN STYLE RIBS

SERVINGS:
Dependent on the amount of ribs used. (One pound of ribs makes approximately 2 servings.)

INGREDIENTS:
Beef or pork ribs
Marinade:
1 c. ketchup
1 c. low sodium soy sauce
1 c. juice (orange for a sweet/tart taste, or pineapple, apple or any juice that you prefer)
2 Tbsp. Worcestershire sauce
½ c. brown sugar
1Tbsp. chopped ginger (fresh or pre-chopped)
3-5 cloves chopped garlic
1 star anise
½ medium onion- chopped in chunks
Fresh ground pepper

Optional:

4 oz. crushed pineapple (if using, cut the sugar in half)
Chopped scallions

PREP NOTES:
Ribs can be cooked in a slow cooker.

If roasting or grilling, parboil ribs to tenderize them and to help infuse the marinade and prep ribs 24 hours in advance.

If your ribs are not pre-cut into single pieces, cut them to make cooking and marinating easier.

If you bought a slab of ribs, before you cut them, turn them over and look for a silvery-white membrane. If you find one, peel the membrane off. The ribs will be more tender this way.

STEPS:
1. Mix all of the marinade ingredients in a bowl.

Slow cooker:
2. Add the ribs to the cooker and cover with marinade. If you have extra, set aside.

3. Slow cook 6 hours on low or 4 hours on high.

Optional:
If you like browned ribs, broil for 10 minutes after cooking, or toss them on the grill until brown.

Boil any remaining marinade for 5-10 minutes (until the onion and garlic are soft) to use as a sauce when serving.

Roasting:
2. Parboil the ribs with onion, salt and pepper in a pot big enough to cover the ribs with water. Bring to a boil over high heat and boil 3-5 minutes, then lower the heat to low and cook for 45 minutes.

3. Place parboiled ribs in a container big enough to hold them.

Cover with marinade and set in refrigerator for 24 hours. Stir once or twice during the 24 hours. (You can marinate for 8-10 hours if you prefer.)

4. When you are ready to cook, preheat oven to 350°F.

5. Remove ribs from marinade and place in a roasting pan.

6. Cook in a pre-heated, 350°F oven for 30 minutes or until browned.

Note:
If you do not want to parboil, marinate the ribs as above, lower the oven temp to 325°F, , and increase the cooking time to 2 hours.

Grilling:
2. Parboil the ribs with onion, salt and pepper in a pot big enough to cover the ribs with water. Bring to a boil over high heat and boil 3-5 minutes, then lower the heat to low and cook for 90 minutes.

3. Place parboiled ribs in a container big enough to hold them. Cover with marinade and set in refrigerator for 24 hours. Stir once or twice during the 24 hours. (You can marinate for 8-10 hours if you prefer.)

4. Grill over medium high heat for 10-12 minutes, turning once.

TOFU STIR FRY

This dish can be eaten alone, or served over rice, oriental noodles, thin spaghetti, etc.

INGREDIENTS:

1 14 oz. container extra firm tofu
Cornstarch
4 carrots (either whole carrots that you can slice into rounds or pre-sliced carrot coins)
1 pepper (any color though yellow or red will add more color)
2 baby bok choy (Chinese cabbage)
1 head broccoli (florets and the stem, or florets only)
2 stalks celery
2-3 cloves garlic
1 c. snow peas
4 oz. mushrooms (any kind)
1 small can water chestnuts
Oil (any type except a heavy olive oil)
Low sodium soy sauce
Splash of rice wine
Salt and pepper

Pinch of sugar
Vegetable broth

Optional variations:
Substitute shrimp for the tofu
Oyster sauce
Star anise
Chinese five spice powder
Chili flakes

PREP NOTES:
If serving with rice or noodles:
Cook before proceeding to the steps below. Cook according to the instructions on the product's package. Tip: Cook rice or noodles in broth rather than water.
Drain the tofu well and pat dry with paper towels. Season with pepper and any spices desired. Toss in a bag or dish to coat with cornstarch.
Vegetable prep:
Note: Try to keep the veggies roughly the same size so that they cook evenly. Try to mix the shapes and sizes to make a prettier plate.
Cut carrots into thin ovals if not precut.
Cut the peppers into strips.
Roughly chop the bok choy.
Separate the broccoli florets. If you want to use the stems, peel and roughly chop them.
Trim the celery and slice the stalks on the diagonal so that they look like a "U" when cut.
Chop the garlic finely.
Trim the ends of the snow peas, making sure that there are no strings.
Slice the mushrooms.
Drain the water chestnuts.

STEPS:

1. Add 1 Tbsp. of oil (or use cooking spray) to a pan (or use a wok if you have one) and bring to temperature over medium heat.

2. Add tofu to pan and cook 7-9 minutes or until golden. Remove from pan and set aside.

3. Add the soy sauce, a splash of rice wine, salt and pepper, sugar and if you like more sauce, add the broth to a bowl. Taste and adjust seasonings. Add any of the optional seasonings that you like.

4. Bring pan back to temperature, medium to medium high, adding a small amount of oil if needed.

5. Add all of the veggies to the pan, except the water chestnuts as they only need to warm and should be added right before the veggies are done.

6. Cook veggies 5 minutes, tossing once or twice.

7. Add sauce and chestnuts. Cook another 5-7 minutes until crisp tender, stirring once or twice.

8. Remove star anise (if used) before serving.

SHOYU CHICKEN

INGREDIENTS:

1/2 c. soy sauce

1/2 c. brown sugar

1/2 c. water

2 cloves garlic, minced

½ medium onion, chopped

½ Tbsp. Worcestershire sauce

½ Tbsp. grated fresh ginger

1 star anise

½ Tbsp. ground black pepper- I prefer fresh ground (You can find small pre-filled grinders in the spice aisle).

½ Tbsp. dried oregano

½ tsp. crushed red pepper flakes (optional)

½ tsp. ground cayenne pepper (optional)

½ tsp. ground paprika

2½ lb. skinless chicken thighs (chicken breasts can be used, but the flavor will not be as rich.)

STEPS:
Slow Cooker/Crock-Pot:

1. Add all of the ingredients (except the chicken) to the cooker and give them a quick stir, leaving the star anise whole so it is easier to remove later.

2. Add the chicken.

3. Cover the cooker and cook on low 6 hours.

Oven:
1. Preheat to 350°F.

2. Add all of the ingredients to a large bowl or a very large zipper bag. Stir or shake to mix, and then add chicken.

3. Let the chicken marinate in the refrigerator for at least 2 hours (or longer to develop the flavor).

4. Remove chicken from marinade. Place in baking pan and cook 45-60 minutes.

Grill:
1. Pre-heat grill, either oil the grate or cover with foil. If using foil, poke holes in the foil with a fork.

2. Add all of the ingredients to a large bowl or a very large zipper bag. Stir or shake to mix, and then add chicken.

3. Let the chicken marinate in the refrigerator for at least 2 hours (or longer to develop the flavor).

4. Remove chicken from marinade. Place on grill and cook 15 minutes per side- turning once.

Instant Pot:

1. Add all ingredients (except chicken) to Instant Pot and stir.

2. Add chicken.

3. Following the directions for your particular model, cook on high 10 minutes.

Stovetop:
1. Add all ingredients (except chicken) to a large pot over med-high heat. Stir till sugar dissolves.

2. Add chicken and bring to a boil.

3. Boil 2 minutes, then reduce heat to low. Simmer 1½ hours till fork tender.

SERVING SUGGESTION:
When done, serve over white rice, brown rice (cooked according to package directions), or riced cauliflower.

SAIMIN RECIPE

Prep and cook time:
Approximately 30 minutes

Servings:
Serves 3-6 (depending on whether it is a side or main dish and how many add-ins you choose.)

INGREDIENTS:
4 qt. water, salted and seasoned with salt, onion powder, and/or garlic powder
1 8-oz. pkg. dried Japanese soba noodles
4 c. chicken broth/stock, vegetable broth/stock, or fish broth/stock
1 Tbsp. grated fresh ginger
2 Tbsp. soy sauce
Fresh ground black pepper to taste
Green onions (or scallions) for garnish
Optional add-ins:
(Mix and match based on your broth and what you have on-hand.)
1 can baby shrimp well-rinsed

Chopped SPAM
Cooked pork
4-5 thinly sliced radishes
Small bunch of thinly sliced bok choy (or baby bok) rinsed well
Matchstick (thinly) cut carrots

Add other items based on your preferences and what you have available.

STEPS:
1. In a large pot over medium-high heat, add 4 quarts of water and salt and bring to a boil.

2. Add soba noodles and boil 4 to 6 minutes until al dente.

3. Remove from heat, drain, and rinse under warm, running water, then drain well again.

4. In a large pot over medium-high heat, add broth/stock and ginger and bring just to a boil.

5. Reduce heat to low.

6. Add soy sauce and any of your favorite veggies and other add-ins.

7. Simmer for 5 minutes longer or until cooked. (Veggies should still be a bit crunchy.)

8. Remove from heat.

9. Place cooked soba noodles in a bowl large enough to hold all of the goodies but wide enough so that you can see all the colors.

10. Pour broth/stock mixture (with toppings) over the top and serve.

AHI POKE

A delicious raw fish salad packed with nutrition that is also low calorie.

Recipe can easily be cut in half for smaller servings.

INGREDIENTS:
2 lb. fresh ahi tuna
1 small round onion, julienne cut (Maui onions preferred)
3 green onions, diced
½ tsp. freshly grated fresh ginger
3 finely diced garlic cloves
½ c. soy sauce
1 tsp. sesame oil
½ tsp. crushed red pepper flakes
1 tsp. Chinese chili sauce (Rooster Brand)
1 tsp. alaea (Hawaiian sea salt) or any other type of sea salt

STEPS:
1. Toss all ingredients in a bowl.

2. Chill until ready to serve.

MANGO OR PINEAPPLE SALSA

Can be used as a topping for fish or can be served with chips.

INGREDIENTS:

1 c. pineapple, diced and drained well
1 mango, diced (or 2 mangoes if omitting the pineapple)
½ c. red bell pepper, diced (or for lots of color, mix red/yellow/orange or green sweet peppers)
2 tsp. of chopped fresh or canned jalapeno (or more to taste)
2 Tbsp. Maui onion (or sweet onion) diced (or fresh spring green onions)
1 Tbsp. sweet chili sauce (Mae Ploy or any other brand)
2 tsp. fresh lime juice (or you can use lemon, or both)
¼-½ tsp. salt to taste (Himalayan Pink Salt, Hawaiian or other sea salt)
2-4 Tbsp. chopped cilantro
Optional:
Use ⅛ tsp. fresh grated ginger (or the one in the tube. Do not used dried or candied ginger.)

STEPS:

1. Mix all ingredients in a large bowl.

2. Cover and refrigerate overnight, if possible. Stir once or twice.

Note:
Do not discard the liquid that forms in the bowl, as that will be used if you are using the salsa as a topping for fish.

FRIED CHICKEN HAWAIIAN STYLE

INGREDIENTS:
4 lb. chicken drumettes
¼ c. flour
½ c. cornstarch
2 eggs
2 stalks green onions, chopped
1-2 garlic cloves, minced
⅓ c. soy sauce
1 Tbsp. sesame seeds
½ tsp. red pepper flakes (or to taste)

***Optional*:**
Omit the red pepper and use fresh ground black pepper and some paprika.

STEPS:
1. Combine all the ingredients in a large bowl.

2. Add chicken to mixture and stir together.

3. Cover bowl and place in refrigerator to marinate 4-6 hours or overnight.

4. When ready to cook, remix, since the batter may separate overnight.

To fry:
1. Using a deep skillet or Dutch oven, add oil about ⅓ of the way full. (Do not use too much oil.)

2. Heat oil to 350°F. (Use a thermometer.)

3. Cook a few pieces at a time (so that you have room to turn them safely) for 10-14 minutes, turning once.

Note:
Be sure that oil returns to 350°F between each batch or the chicken will not cook fully or will be soggy.

To partially fry/bake:
1. Follow instructions above, but decrease cooking time to 5 to 8 minutes, turning once.

2. Finish by baking in a 350°F oven for 15-20 minutes, depending on size.

See tip below.

To bake:
1. Allow excess batter to drip off of chicken.

2. Space chicken pieces well apart on a baking sheet, pizza pan, or jellyroll pan. Place cookie/cake cooling racks in the pan. Spray lightly with cooking spray or wipe them with a tiny bit of oil to

keep chicken from sticking. (Using the racks allows air and heat all around chicken and that is where the crispiness comes from. It also allows excess grease to drain.) Do not crowd them, for best results.

3. Bake in 425°F oven 20-30 minutes, depending on size.

To air fry:
1. Spray basket lightly.

2. Allow excess batter to drip off of chicken. Work in small batches, do not crowd. As air fryers vary in size and power, follow the instructions in your air fryer's manual. Most will be set from 360-390°F and the time will vary. Be sure to turn chicken. You can keep the batches warm using the tip below- just set your oven to warm)or the lowest setting).

Tip for oven warming/crisping:
Use a baking sheet/pizza or jelly roll pan. Place cookie/cake cooling racks in the pan. Spray lightly with cooking spray or wipe them with a tiny bit of oil to keep chicken from sticking. Using the racks allows air and heat all around chicken and that is where the crispiness comes from. It also allows excess grease to drain.

HAWAIIAN PASTA SALAD

INGREDIENTS:
1/2 of a 16-ounce box/bag of shaped pasta-
14 oz can of pineapple drained but save the juice
1 medium pepper – chopped
16 oz of good quality ham or shrimp
1/2 cup of diced celery
1/4 cup finely chopped onion
1/2 cup shredded carrots
Dressing:
1/4 cup sour cream (reg or low fat)
1/2 cup mayonnaise
1 tsp horseradish
1 tsp red wine vinegar (tastes best) or apple cider vinegar
1 tsp sugar or honey
1/3 cup pineapple juice (from the canned fruit above)- add slowly
and taste often
Onion/garlic powder- to taste
Pepper (fresh ground if possible) - to taste
Optional add-ins or garnishes:
Grape or cherry tomatoes. Chop fine

Fresh shredded coconut
Macadamia nuts, chopped

STEPS:

1. Cook the pasta according to the directions on the box. Al dente is best as the pasta will absorb some moisture from the dressing.

2. Drain the pineapple well by letting it sit in a drainer for a few minutes, then let it sit on a paper towel for a few minutes more. Save the juice.

3. In a big bowl, toss together the pasta, pineapple, pepper, ham (or shrimp), celery, onions and carrots.

4. In a separate bowl, stir the remaining ingredients together and pour over the pasta mixture and stir to mix.

5. Chill 4-6 hours, and stir gently once or twice to keep pasta coated.

6. Serve in a bowl or on a plate.

Note:

To make it elegant, use Boston/Bibb lettuce or whole romaine leaves as a dish. Top with optional ingredients or place them in separate bowls and let everyone choose their own toppings.

SPAM MUSUBI

All ingredients should be easy to find in your grocery store or local Asian market.

PREP:
Cook the rice ahead of time so it cools.
INGREDIENTS:
1 12-oz. can Spam
6 Tbsp. soy sauce
4 Tbsp. mirin (Japanese sweet rice wine)- optional, but adds a nice flavor.
4 Tbsp. sugar (or your favorite sugar substitute)
4 to 5 sheets of nori seaweed, cut in half the long way
5 c. cooked sushi rice, cooled (roughly 1½ c. rice before cooking)
Furikake Japanese seasoning, any flavor

Optional:
Li Hing Mui- salty dried plum powder
Sesame seeds

STEPS:

Notes:

You will need a clean, flat surface to work on.

You will need a musubi maker or a clean Spam can with both ends cut off. (Place bottom in a small amount of water to keep wet.)

1. Cut the Spam lengthwise into 8-10 equal slices.

2. Place Spam slices in pan and fry until lightly crisp. (You can grill the slices but be very gentle.) If you do not use a non-stick pan, use oil or spray as needed. If you use oil, be sure to drain the slices on a paper towel or paper plate, then return the slices to the pan.

3. In a small saucepan, bring the soy sauce, mirin and sugar to a boil, then lower heat and add the Spam slices, turning once gently.

4. Cook Spam until the sauce is thickened.

5. Remove Spam from pan and set aside on a plate.

6. Place a sheet of nori on flat surface- lengthwise, shiny side down, rough side up. Think of the nori sheet in thirds, placing the maker/can at either end (⅓ of your sheet).

7. Fill the maker/can ⅓ high with rice and press down hard until rice is tightly packed.

8. Sprinkle rice with furikake (or Li Hing Mui) and sesame seeds.

9. Top with Spam slice and press down lightly.

10. Top with more rice, pressing down to pack rice.

11. Top with more sesame seeds.

12. Carefully remove maker/can, so as not to break the stack, then return maker/can to water.

13. Wrap the stack with the nori.

14. Dampen the end of the nori to seal it, just as you would ravioli or pie dough.

15. Repeat the above steps to make the rest of the *musubi*.

16. If you aren't eating them right away, wrap tightly in plastic wrap.

Note:
Musubi can be made with any additional ingredients that you like, such as chicken or hot dogs.

KALUA PORK

This recipe can be made in the slow cooker (8 -10 hours on low) or in the oven (3 hours at 375°F.) Use a deep roasting pan. If you use a smaller roast, check for doneness 1 hour before stated times above.

INGREDIENTS:
4-5 lb. pork shoulder or pork butt, fat on. (If there is a lot of fat, you can trim some, but this is what keeps the meat moist.)
2 tsp.-2 Tbsp. alaea (Hawaiian sea salt) or any other sea salt.
Banana leaves or cabbage leaves, or aluminum foil, enough to wrap your roast
4 Tbsp. liquid smoke
6 c. water

Notes:
You can sometimes find Hawaiian sea salt in the Northeast US at Marshalls, TJ Maxx and gourmet food stores.
You can sometimes find banana leaves at a florist or Asian market. (If you don't want to use cabbage or banana leaves, you can wrap

the roast VERY tightly in aluminum foil before putting it in the roasting pan.)

STEPS:

1. Place banana or cabbage leaves in the bottom and up the sides of your slow cooker or roasting pan, or wrap the roast tightly in aluminum foil if you do not want to use banana or cabbage leaves.

2. Score (pierce with a fork or knife) the fatty side of the roast.

3. Place the roast in the pan on top of the leaves or wrapped in foil.

4. Add the liquid smoke and pat on the salt.

5. Then cover the roast with more leaves (if applicable) and wrap tightly.

6. In the slow cooker, add ½ to 1 cup of water; in a roasting pan, add enough water to come halfway up the sides of the pan.

7. Serve the meat shredded with sticky (or any rice), sweet potatoes, sauteed cabbage, macaroni salad, chunky applesauce, or any of your favorite sides.

FRESH HAWAIIAN FISH

SERVINGS:
4 servings

SERVING SUGGESTION:
Fish can be served with rice, used in fish tacos (using shells/tortillas and add-ins), with a nice sweet and sour slaw or traditional coleslaw, or your favorite side.

INGREDIENTS:
1½ lb. fish (Mahi Mahi is the first choice; however, if you can't find it, use any light white fish.)
Salt and pepper
Any favorite fish rub, seasoning, etc.
Extra liquid from the mango/pineapple salsa mixture if it has been made.

Optional:
Crushed macadamia nuts to cover fish
Lemon (to add to fish while cooking and for squeezing over fish when serving)

STEPS:
1. Rinse the fish and pat dry

2. To add flavor to the fish, add the fish to a zip-top bag or bowl and drizzle with some of the liquid from the salsa or slaw, if available.

3. Set aside for an hour or longer if you have time.

4. When ready to cook, remove fish from the liquid. Season with salt, pepper and any other favorite seasoning. If you would like a nice crust on the fish, roll it in crushed macadamia nuts. The secret to a good crust is to chill the fish for an hour in the refrigerator to firm the crust, then cook it. If you skip this step, you will still get a crust but not as firm.

For oven or grill packets:
5. Cut a piece of heavy duty foil twice as large as the fish. Spray lightly with cooking spray or use a tiny amount of oil to keep the fish from sticking.

6. Lay the fish on the foil (adding a lemon slice if you like) and fold into a packet, crimping the sides well.

For oven cooking:
5. Cook fish in 350°F oven for 30-35 minutes, or until fish flakes easily with a fork.

For grill cooking:
You can use a grill basket instead of a foil packet, but be sure to coat the basket with cooking spray or oil.

5. Preheat the grill to medium-high heat.

6. Place packet (or basket) on grill.

7. Cook fish for 10-15 minutes, depending on thickness, until fish flakes with a fork.

For stovetop cooking:
5. Spray a large skillet with cooking spray or use a small amount of oil to coat pan and preheat on med-high.

6. Add fish to pan and cook 6 minutes on each side, turning only once. (Adjust time based on thickness.)

SWEET THINGS

PINEAPPLE BANANA BREAD

SERVINGS:
Makes 1 loaf.

INGREDIENTS:
1½ c. flour
⅓ tsp. salt
½ tsp. baking soda
1 c. sugar
½ tsp. cinnamon
⅛ tsp. nutmeg
⅛ tsp. ground ginger
½ c. chopped macadamia nuts
2 eggs, beaten
1 tsp. vanilla
½ c. crushed pineapple, drained
½ c. oil (vegetable, canola- any healthy non-flavored oil), or ½ c.
unsweetened applesauce
¾ c. mashed banana (Suggest bananas that are going brown, as
they have better consistency and flavor.)

PREP:

This recipe can be made in one loaf pan, a couple of mini-loaf pans, or as cupcakes. Grease and flour your pan of choice.

Preheat oven to 350°F.

STEPS:

1. In a large bowl, add all the dry ingredients and stir well.

2. Add nuts and stir to coat. (This keeps them from sinking while baking.)

Note:
You can mix the dry and wet ingredients separately in another bowl, then combine them, which makes it easier to get all the wet ingredients incorporated. Either way works.

3. Add eggs and vanilla and stir well.

4. Add pineapple, oil and banana.

5. Stir until all ingredients are well combined and there are no lumps of flour. (This will be a thick batter.)

6. Pour into pan and bake at 350°F for 60 minutes. (If using a loaf pan, check doneness with a toothpick after 45 minutes. If using mini-loaf pans or cupcake tins, check with toothpick after 30 minutes. Bread is done when toothpick comes out clean.)

Optional:
Prior to baking, top the batter with chopped cherries, drained, or shredded coconut.

MANGO BREAD

SERVINGS:
Makes 1 loaf

PREP:
This recipe can be made in one loaf pan, a couple of mini-loaf pans, or as cupcakes. Grease and flour your pan of choice.

Preheat oven to 350°F.

INGREDIENTS:
2 c. flour
2 tsp. baking soda
1 tsp. salt
1 c. sugar
1 tsp. cinnamon
½ c. dried cranberries or raisins
¾ c. vegetable oil (Use any healthy non-flavored oil or 3/4 c. unsweetened applesauce.
3 eggs
2 c. chopped ripe mangos

1 tsp. vanilla extract

STEPS:

1. In a large bowl, add all of the dry ingredients and stir well.

2. Add cranberries/raisins and stir to coat.

3. Add mango and stir well to coat. (This keeps them from sinking while baking.)

Note:
You can mix the dry and wet ingredients separately and then combine them, which makes it easier to get all of the wet ingredients incorporated. Either way works.

4. Add oil, eggs and vanilla.

5. Stir all ingredients until well combined and there are no lumps of flour. (This will be a very thick batter.)

6. Pour into pan and bake. (If using a loaf pan, bake 60 minutes but check with toothpick after 45 minutes. If using mini-loaf pans or cupcake tins, check with toothpick after 30 minutes. Bread is done when toothpick comes out clean.)

Optional:
Prior to baking, top the batter with chopped strawberries, shredded coconut or chopped nuts.

HULA PIE

Make this a day ahead of serving for best results.

SERVINGS:
Makes 1 pie

INGREDIENTS:
4 oz. chocolate fudge topping at room temperature (homemade or from a jar)
1½ oz. espresso, strong coffee, or milk
½ gal. macadamia nut ice cream (If not available, use vanilla bean ice cream.)
1 c. chopped macadamia nuts
1 chocolate cookie pie crust

STEPS:
1. Let ice cream soften so that it is scoopable and moundable, but still firm enough to hold its shape. (If using vanilla bean ice cream, stir in ¾ of the nuts.)

2. Check to ensure that there are no cracks in your pie shell.

3. Scoop the ice cream into the pie shell. It should be even with the pie shell at the edge and mounded in the center.

4. Thin the topping with the espresso, coffee or milk and pour the topping over the center of the mound, letting it drip down.

5. Sprinkle with the rest of the chopped nuts.

6. Place in freezer until fully solid, overnight if possible.

For a single serving (enough for 2 to share):
1. Crush 2 or 3 chocolate wafers (the Nabisco brand work best) into the bottom of a ramekin or small dish.

2. Top the wafers with 2 scoops of ice cream, mounding in the center.

3. Cover with fudge sauce and nuts and freeze.

HAWAIIAN PINEAPPLE CAKE

Note: *This recipe requires use of a candy thermometer.*

INGREDIENTS:
Batter:
2 c. flour
1½ c. granulated sugar
3 tsp. baking powder
1 tsp. salt
⅓ c. shortening
1 c. milk
½ tsp. lemon flavoring
½ tsp. vanilla extract
2 egg yolks + 1 whole egg
Pineapple Filling:
½ c. granulated sugar
3 Tbsp. cornstarch
½ tsp. salt
¾ c. pineapple juice
1 c. crushed pineapple

1 Tbsp. butter
1 tsp. lemon juice

White Mountain Frosting:
¾ c. granulated sugar
3 Tbsp. water
¼ c. light corn syrup
3 egg whites
1½ tsp. vanilla

STEPS:
Cake:
1. Blend flour, sugar, baking powder, and salt.

2. Add shortening, ⅔ c. milk, lemon flavoring, and vanilla extract.

3. Beat 2 minutes.

4. Add remaining milk and eggs. Beat 2 minutes more.

5. Butter and flour 2 round cake pans and divide batter evenly between them. You can also cut a piece of parchment paper to fit the bottoms of the pans to help get the cake out more easily.

6. Bake at 350°F for 30-35 minutes, testing for doneness with a toothpick inserted in the center. If the cakes are done, the toothpick should come out clean.

7. When done, remove the cakes from the oven and cool completely.

8. Remove from pans, dusting away any crumbs. If your cake has crowned or domed, use a serrated knife to even up the top of one of the layers. This will help the top and bottom layer to sit better.

Filling:

1. Mix sugar, cornstarch, and salt in saucepan.

2. Gradually stir in juices.

3. Bring to a boil and boil for one minute.

4. Remove from heat.

5. Stir in butter.

6. Stir in pineapple after mixture has cooled.

7. Spread filling between the two cake layers. Try not to go all the way to the edges, as this may cause the filling to leak out while you are trying to frost your cake.

Frosting:

1. Mix sugar, water, and corn syrup in saucepan.

2. Bring to a boil and, using a candy thermometer, heat to 242°F.

3. Remove from heat.

4. Beat egg whites in mixing bowl until stiff.

5. Pour hot syrup from saucepan into beaten egg whites.

6. Beat mixture until frosting holds peaks.

7. Frost top and sides of cake.

8. Let sit for a few minutes to set.

9. Serve, and enjoy!

ACKNOWLEDGMENTS

Dear Readers,

I hope you enjoyed this uplifting story that celebrates some of the best of human nature!

The recipes project from foods mentioned in the book was a ton of fun to assemble. I asked readers to submit their favorite Hawaiian recipes in my Friends Who Like Toby Neal Books Facebook group. (Join us there for lots of ongoing shenanigans!)

Erin Finigan, a terrific cook, undertook to kitchen test, vary, and rewrite all of these recipes included so that they don't violate any copyrights. You can cook these wonderful dishes knowing they've been "road-tested" by the best!

I greatly enjoyed returning to explore Aunty Rosario's world at *Aunty's Hawaiian Food Place*, giving new backstory about her and her big heart. I hope to include the kids in this story in some future book, all grown-up and contributing to the fabric of their communities and this great nation.

Thanks so much for being on this journey with Lei and all of her growing '*ohana*!' Look for exciting new additions to her Paradise Crime Mystery world in the year to come!

Much aloha,

FREE BOOKS

Join my mystery and romance lists and receive free, full-length, award-winning novels *Torch Ginger & Somewhere on St. Thomas.*

tobyneal.net/TNNews

TOBY'S BOOKSHELF

PARADISE CRIME SERIES

Paradise Crime Mysteries
Blood Orchids

Torch Ginger

Black Jasmine

Broken Ferns

Twisted Vine

Shattered Palms

Dark Lava

Fire Beach

Rip Tides

Bone Hook

Red Rain

Bitter Feast

Razor Rocks

Paradise Crime Mysteries Novella
Clipped Wings

Paradise Crime Mystery
Special Agent Marcella Scott
Stolen in Paradise

Paradies Crime Suspense Mysteries
Unsound

Paradise Crime Thrillers
Wired In
Wired Rogue
Wired Hard
Wired Dark
Wired Dawn
Wired Justice
Wired Secret
Wired Fear
Wired Courage
Wired Truth

ROMANCES
Toby Jane

The Somewhere Series
Somewhere on St. Thomas
Somewhere in the City
Somewhere in California
Somewhere in Wine Country
(Coming 2020)

Standalone
Somewhere on Maui

Co-Authored Romance Thrillers
The Scorch Series

Scorch Road
Cinder Road
Smoke Road
Burnt Road
Flame Road
Smolder Road

YOUNG ADULT

Standalone
Island Fire

NONFICTION

Memoir
Freckled

ABOUT THE AUTHOR

Kirkus Reviews calls Neal's writing, *"persistently riveting. Masterly."*

Award-winning, USA Today bestselling social worker turned author Toby Neal grew up on the island of Kaua`i in Hawaii. Neal is a mental health therapist, a career that has informed the depth and complexity of the characters in her stories. Neal's mysteries and thrillers explore the crimes and issues of Hawaii from the bottom of the ocean to the top of volcanoes. Fans call her stories, *"Immersive, addicting, and the next best thing to being there."*

Neal also pens romance, romantic thrillers, and writes memoir/nonfiction under TW Neal.

Visit tobyneal.net for more ways to stay in touch!
or
Join my Facebook readers group, *Friends Who Like Toby Neal Books,* for special giveaways and perks.

Made in the USA
Middletown, DE
06 February 2024

49206528R00097